ESCAPE FROM HELL!

Escape from Hell!

Hal Duncan

To my amigo in madness, Mags,
for the blitzkrieg brainstorming sessions,
the beers and banter, the cocktails and craic.
Bless ye!

PROLOGUE

Night in the City

It's night in the city, clouds overhead painted crimson by the streetlights, roof underfoot mirroring the same light in the sleek of water shattered by splash-patterns of ripples and raindrops, constant but arrhythmic, out of synch with the slow onward trudge of bootsteps—left, right—through the puddles of liquid night—left, right—stepping up to a low wall's edge—left, right—and onto it. Left. Right.

Look down. Pull back. The alley below is a thin chasm of darkness patched by windows to the left, a neon sign at the corner, sliced for a second as a sword of light sweeps the rain. The beam of a police copter's searchlight picks out a shamble of ragged coats which was once a man named Eli, standing now on the edge of nameless death, a vagrant suicide in the city morgue. His arms are spread as he testifies to the copter, St John Doe the Divine.

– And I looked, he shouts, and behold, the heavens opened. And I saw a great white throne, and He who sat upon it, from whose face even the earth and the heaven fled away.

Loudspeaker noise urges him back from the edge, but he doesn't listen to the words, just looks over his shoulder back the way he came. The wind that's been batting the open fire exit door against concrete finally lets it go. The door swings slowly shut as Eli turns back to his little back-alley abyss.

\#

In the emptiness of the warehouse, the sound of the bullet being chambered in the Desert Eagle echoes loud and clear. Israeli gun designed to scare the shit out of a

I

man before it's even fired, to tell you: Listen up, fucker; that's the sound of your death coming down upon you. Seven raises his head, angles it back until he feels it touch the gun-barrel.

– Go ahead, motherfucker, he says. If T-Bone wanted me dead, you wouldn't be wasting your time with this bullshit.

Too-Loose and Hound Dogg are Desert Eagles in the shape of men, heavy pressure rather than precision hitters. So their contract won't be for a quick disposal; they'll have something slower and more painful lined up for Seven. Too-Loose circles round to stand in front of him, gun aimed at Seven's face, then lowering to his chest, his gut, his balls.

– You blew a contract, Seven, says Hound Dogg at his ear. T-Bone got to make an example of you. We're gonna do a lot more than just kill you, nigger.

His arms behind his back, Seven's fingers test the handcuffs as the man talks: two pairs, police-issue, one cuff on each wrist, the other looping a back leg and corner of the chair he's sat on. He curls his hand up, reaching with index and forefinger, almost manages to tease the pin from the cuff of his right sleeve—almost but not quite. It slips from his fingers, falls to the ground. He looks up to meet Too-Loose's gaze without blinking, even smiling a little, just enough to make the thug twitch a tiny sign of contempt, somewhere between a narrowing of an eye and a curl of an upper lip. The man switches the gun to his other hand and reaches into the pocket of his leather jacket, brings his fist out brass-knuckled.

– You're not gonna be smiling long, Seven, he says.

He puts his whole body behind the punch.

#

The backhand knocks Belle to one side, against the wall;

she slaps a hand against it to keep from falling, but he's grabbing her hair and pulling her back for another slap.

– Where you going, bitch?

– Nowhere, she says. Nowhere, Johnny.

The half-packed suitcase on the bed says otherwise. The open drawers and closets say otherwise. So did the fear on her face when he walked in through the door of the apartment.

– You fucking running out on me, Belle?

He hits her backhand again, contemptuous, casual, like he's kicking a cowed dog. And why not? That's what she is, after all, a fucking cowed dog, a pimp's bitch. She wants to stand up for herself, but she backs away, hands up to shield her face. There's no smell of drink on him, but his eyes are bullet holes, his shoulders stuck in a shrug, his hands matching his verbal anger with their own wild rhythms.

– Fucking no one fucking runs out on me, he says, fucking bitch.

She ducks back from his swing, dodging, hears his curse as the punch connects with wall. She dodges past him for the open door, but he hauls her back, swings her hard into the dresser. Bottles of cheap perfume and cologne scatter and roll as it judders.

– You're going fucking nowhere, he says.

Another backhand, angled down and hard enough to knock her to the floor. She looks up and, through the hair over her eyes, sees him walk over to the apartment door, close it with a quiet menace.

#

The double-doors bounce open into the ER, orderlies wheeling in the gurney, paramedics to this side, doctors to that, talking across the bloodied mess, rattling a litany of injuries and assessments. Matthew doesn't hear, doesn't know that he has:

3

– primary hypothermia, stage three—temperature eighty-eight degrees Fahrenheit—blunt cranial trauma in the left occipital region—lacerations—abrasions—contusions—noticeable ecchymoses on the right and left rib cage—hematoma on the abdomen, feels like internal hemorrhage on the spleen—a fracture to the left femur—numerous small third degree burns in right scapular region, probably from a cigarette…

Matthew doesn't know that he's in critical condition, naked and blue with the cold from being stripped and left in winter snow, that he's been cut and kicked and pistol-whipped, that he's bleeding and burned and broken-boned, not now.

– Rapid infusion of 250 mils lactated Ringer's solution, stat.

He doesn't know that his blond hair is matted, that his face is smeared with blood, his square jaw broken, features swollen and cracked from a pounding he doesn't remember, not now.

Being beaten to death can have that effect.

The gurney bangs through another set of double doors.

#

The Sound of Many Rivers

Eli digs into his pocket for a bottle—bourbon, nearly done. He slugs back what's left and raises the empty to the searchlit rain, the copter, the sound of rotor blades and loudspeaker.

– And I heard a great thunder from heaven, he shouts, like the sound of many rivers, like the sound of harpists playing on their harps. And I heard a loud voice out of heaven saying, behold, God's house has come unto his people, and he will dwell with them, and God himself will be their king.

He hurls the bottle out into the chasm of the alley.

#

– I own you, get it?

   – I get it. I do. I'm sorry.

But even as she tries to calm him, he's feeling the bulge in her jacket pocket, pulling out the roll of bills she's been gathering for the last few months. He pulls her head back by the hair.

   – You holding out on me, Belle?

   – No, Johnny, I've just been saving.

Then the punch crumples her legs and she's on the floor, trying to push herself away, finding a wall behind her.

#

– Look at this nigger trying to crawl away, Hound Dogg laughs. You don't know you're a dead man already, Seven?

   Seven, on the floor and on his side, still cuffed to the chair, pushes with his feet. Just another inch and he feels the pick with his fingertips, another inch and—

Too-Loose and Hound Dogg grab him by the shoulders, haul him up, kick the chair back into place beneath him. Hound Dogg's pistol cracks across his face, but Seven has the pick in his fingers, working at the cuff holding his right wrist to the chair. Too-Loose clamps his hands on his shoulders, holds him down as Hound Dogg, puts his gun into its shoulder holster, brings a flick-knife out of his inside pocket. Clicks it open.

   – Dead man, he says. We just gotta cut you open to find the cause.

#

They wheel Matthew into the O.R.—three, two, one— and heave him onto the table. There's a tube being pushed into his throat, a needle into his arm, lights overhead, wires everywhere hooking him up to monitors, a doctor scanning his paperwork, handing it to a nurse.

– Blood pressure falling to eighty over forty.

Matthew knows none of this.

– We've got cardiac arrhythmia, ventricular fibrillation.

He's not really here right now.

– AED.

Not that he's anywhere else.

– Charge to two hundred joules.

Not yet.

– All clear.

#

A Small White Light

– And the sea gave up the dead that were in it, Eli preaches to the rain and light. Death and Hell gave up the dead that were in them. I saw the dead, the great and the small, standing before the throne, each with a book held in their hand. And they were judged, each one, out of the things which were written in the books.

He reaches, brings a battered Bible out of his jacket, fumbles through its pages to find a photograph of the man he once was, standing there with his arm around Sarah, Sarah's hand on the shoulder of their little girl, Lucy, smiling there between them. The Bible slips from his hand and he staggers a little as he tries to catch it, fails. He's drunk, he knows, too drunk to hold onto a book or to care about picking it up. And just about drunk enough for this.

#

Left hand still cuffed, as he rises Seven swings the chair out from beneath him, cracks Hound Dogg with it, full in the face. With his right hand, at the same time, he grabs Too-Loose by the throat. He hauls, curling his back and using the other man's own mass to lever him over his shoulder, bring him down, back-first, upon the edge of the chair's steel seat. He drops to wrap his arm

around the man's neck, snap it with a quick twist, rips Too-Loose's Desert Eagle from his waistband, and rolls the body away. Hound Dogg has his own gun out now, but Seven is already spinning, bringing the chair around to smack it aside, bringing the Desert Eagle up and firing point-blank into Hound Dogg's face.
#

Johnny kicks the words into her.

– This. Is what. You get. For fucking. Trying to. Fucking. *Leave me.*

At first she feels each blow, curled in a ball, his boot beating his message into her body, legs, and forearms; she tries to make herself as small as possible, to plead when she's not crying out from the pain. Then his boot hits her head and it's just light and dark and pain, broken and blurred glimpses of carpet, ceiling, bed, or boot, Johnny standing over her, a jumble of disconnected violence, senseless. She's crawling, falling, grabbing at his legs. If she could just—
#

– No change. He's still arrhythmic.

Somewhere inside Matthew, in the dark, there is a small white light.

– Charge to three hundred.

The light is getting dimmer.

– All clear.
#

Death Will Be No More
– The light of the lamp will shine no more, sobs Eli, for the fruits which your soul lusted after have all perished, and all things that were delicate and beautiful have been lost to you.

Seven walks through the warehouse, down the central aisle, alleys of crates to left and right, the exit a bright blur of daylight straight ahead—the loading bay. Brown leather jacket, gun in each hand, handcuffs dangling from his wrists, he knows there's no point trying to make a quiet exit, knows the only way out now is to be a motherfucking dreadnaught. A worker steps into his path, sees him and turns to run; Seven drops him with a bullet in the back. A man with an Uzi skids into sight at the far end of the aisle, lets off an aimless burst of staccato gunfire as Seven puts two bullets in his chest.

#

– The voices of harpists and singers, flute players and trumpeters will be heard no more. The sound of the craftsmen working will be heard no more.

Down an aisle to his right, Seven spots another foot soldier, hears the crack of his gun, the whine of a bullet flying past his head. Even as he fires and the man drops, Seven keeps on walking.

Belle crawls across the floor, away from the pain, but there's no escaping it. The palm of her hand comes down upon the rosary she wears around her neck, torn off in the beating. She clutches it tight even as Johnny kicks her again, in the ribs, hard enough to send her rolling.

#

– The noise of the mill will be heard no more. The laughter of the bridegroom and of the bride will be heard no more.

Two more, three, *four* foot soldiers appear ahead, take cover. Seven strides on towards them, both guns firing as he pulls the triggers over and over again.

Belle feels her hair ripped out at the roots as Johnny pulls her to her feet. She tries to stand but she can't. She just can't. A hand clamps round her throat, not to strangle her but to hold her up, to spit in her face.

– Charge to three sixty.

In a darkness empty even of pain, Matthew is dying.

– All clear.

#

– But he will wipe away from them every tear from their eyes. Neither will there be mourning, nor crying, nor pain. For Death will be no more.

And Eli spreads his arms out to the rain and the light, to the copter circling him, to God, to the world, to his own pitiful end; and, turning to the darkness of the alley below, he lets himself fall forward—

And Seven strides into a *thud* in his chest he doesn't quite feel until his legs suddenly weaken, and the next step brings him down onto one knee; the guns are just too heavy to keep raised now, shit, it's all he can do to look up at the heavy walking towards him, pistol pointed at his forehead, grinning as he pulls the trigger—

And Belle's legs are rubber as Johnny pushes her away from him; she tries to hold herself up, she does, but she just stumbles over her own feet, falls, head cracking hard against the radiator, all her weight behind it, twisting, snapping bone, and as she slumps to the floor, a length of rosary slides from her open hand—

And the noise of a flatline on a monitor just carries on as the doctor pumps, palm-over-palm on Matthew's chest, trying to restart his silent heart, trying again, and again, and again, until finally he steps back and calls the time of death—

And Eli lies on the ground, the old family photo crumpled in his fist, in a puddle of rainwater darkening with his blood.

#

The Ferry Across the Styx
The sound of a distant foghorn, clang of footsteps on the swaying steel underfoot. Eli opens his eyes. He's on

the car deck of a ferry, he realises, rust-stained paint on metal walls cutting off his view to either side, the great dark slab of the door at his back, chains running down each side from pulleys to spindles, to unwind and lower the door into a ramp. Overhead, the sky is heavy, the formless smudge of a charcoal and chalk sketch left out in the rain.

There are no vehicles on the car deck, just a scattering of strange passengers, an assemblage of men, women, and children of all ages and races, in all manner of clothes—suits or pyjamas, evening wear or combat gear. Most stand awkwardly, gazing around with the unease of the lost, too overawed to ask what the fuck is going on, how they got here. Only here or there, as a few begin to sob or pray, others start to murmur questions to those nearest: Is this a dream?

Eli touches his ragged brown overcoat, just the outer layer of strata of clothing; it's still soaked from the rain, still dripping. He doesn't remember the moment of impact, sudden as it was, too fast to feel, but he knows what's happened to him, what he imagines has happened to them all. He doesn't need anyone to tell him, No, this isn't a dream. This is death.

#

Seven pushes his way through the crowd. This is fucked-up, he thinks. This is some fucked-up amnesia shit. He doesn't know how many days or weeks or months he's lost since somehow he got out of the warehouse, but he can feel that he's not packing, and whatever this... freak show is, it's not anywhere he wants to stay. He pushes past an old man dressed in nothing but his boxers, steps round a little girl in an ice-skating costume, boots dangled round her neck, and makes his way to a set of grilled steps leading to the upper decks. He glances back at the other passengers as he climbs, scouring his mind for an answer. What the fuck are they all doing here dressed like... refugees from some fucking disaster, whatever the fuck *here* is?

There are more passengers on the walkway that overlooks the lower deck, all dressed as crazily as those below, more visible through the windows of an enclosed seating area. It's the sight to starboard that holds his eye now, though. Over the rail, across the chop of a river in winter, through low clouds and mist, is a skyline that looks not unlike Manhattan, but ragged and hollow like every window in the city of skyscrapers was smashed, every building shelled and shot up, every surface painted with dust and ash.

– Holy fuck, says Seven.

#

Belle lets the door into the passenger area swing shut behind her and steps out onto the starboard walkway. Given the muttered oath, it doesn't seem like the brick shithouse with the Black Panther look is any more clued-up than her, but he's the first passenger she's seen not just gaping dumbly at their strange surroundings.

– Where are we? says Belle. You know what's going on?

He barely acknowledges her existence with a glance, something that *might* just be a shake of his head, before he's walking away from her, towards the front of the ferry.

– Fuck you too, she says under her breath.

She heads the other way, sidestepping an old woman in a ball gown, glancing down at the other weirdoes on the car deck, at the shambling hulk of a hobo climbing the port stairs to the upper deck, at the sight over the port rail. She stops. On a small island off the port side stands a grey-green statue, grand in her flowing Grecian robes and spiked crown, sword in her right hand, scales in her left. A blindfold covers her eyes.

– Lady Justice, says a voice at her back, the old woman.

– Where the fuck are we? says Belle.

The old woman cackles, a crazy leer on her face.

– Oh, you know where we are, sweetie. Don't pretend you don't.

Belle backs away from the hag, along the port walkway.

– You *know* where we're going. You *know*.

She points past Belle, ahead, and Belle can't help but turn, eyes caught by the Statue of Justice again for just a second, before catching the sight now coming clear through the mists ahead.

– No, she says. No.

#

Matthew shivers on his wooden bench, naked under the thin green cloth of the surgical sheet stained with what he knows is his own blood. He pays no mind to the other passengers, sitting on benches round the open-air seating area or standing at the rails, looking out at the statue to one side, the city to the other. He stares straight ahead, his fingers flat on the wood as if to support himself, like without his hands on something solid he might just… fall off the world. He's not sure he hasn't already; even the grey river under them seems ethereal, a surface of mist as much as water.

It can't be real. This can't be happening.

In front of him the island is close now, close enough that he can see the guards in grey outside the red brick building grand as a palace, close enough that he can see the Gothic intricacy of the lettering on the iron gates across the dock, swinging open now to admit the ferry, close enough that there's no mistaking the words spelled out. He'd had a moment of panic when he first tried to read them in the distance, certain for a second that the motto was "Arbeit Macht Frei." But now, as the ferry slips in through the gateway, as gears crank and rattle into reverse, as the iron gates swing slowly back together, slowly closing, slowly creaking into place with a low *doom*, now he knows those letters spell a message just as chilling.

Abandon Hope.

ACT ONE-ARRIVAL

This Is Hell

Seven gazes over the rail at the turreted block of the Immigration Building, blood-red brick and ashen concrete, a triple set of double doors for an entrance, each with a glass-panelled arch above, and a larger arch over them all. He notes the guards who line their path from the lowering gangplank of the ferry to this entrance, rows of them, three deep on either side, all armed and all armoured, the uniforms under the Kevlar vests weird-but-familiar, familiar-but-weird—like Homeland Security but in shades of grey instead of black and blue. A squad of them march up the secured gangplank, begin herding the passengers off the boat.

#

Seven goes with the flow—for now, at least, wise to the fact he's in nightmareland, knowing jackshit more than that. He's not about to do anything stupid without a little more… context. From the panic on the faces of the other passengers—refugees, prisoners, whatever—he won't have long to wait, he reckons, to see what happens if you make a break for it.

He's right.

It's an OAP in a leisure suit and gold chain who loses it at the bottom of the gangplank, breaks out of the shuffling mob and starts hollering his outrage, trying to push free. Others join his indignant protests, but Seven just watches as the guards beat the old man down with Taser-ended batons, then move on to the others. He weighs up his own chances, decides the odds aren't in his favour. Not here. Not now.

#

– Keep it moving, please. Come on. In the doors and to

your right. Keep it moving, people. Through the doors and to your right.

Belle shuffles forward with the mob, follows them into the cold tiles of the echoing hall, the steel rail that snakes the queue left and right, thins it to single file. She cranes her neck over the throng to see the far end— walk-through scanners, guards with guns and cameras talking into radios. Ahead of her a young man in a suit nervously approaches one of the guards stationed at points along the queue.

– Please, can you tell us—

The baton smacks across his face. A hand shoves him roughly on.

– No talking, sir. Please, if you'll all just keep the line moving. Just shut the fuck up and move it. Sir.

#

She's swept on through a paranoid nightmare of bureaucracy and security, the insane truth of it circling in her mind, a three-word sentence that blocks all other thought, a sentence that can't be true but which she can't get out of her head. She would be mumbling it over and over to herself except she's way too deep in shock to speak. Instead the words just loop inside her head, the pitch of them rising with her fear, her horror:

This is Hell. This is Hell. This is Hell.

#

The Sigil of His Sin

Eli keeps his head down and does what he's told, moves when he's ordered, says nothing. The queue inches forward, bringing him closer to the rows of conveyor-belt x-ray machines, walk-through metal detectors, guards with hand-held scanners.

– Stop there. You, come forward. Arms like this.

He watches a man in front walk through the gate, stand to be swept, his arms out wide. The guard picks up a plastic bucket.

    – Take off the watch, please, sir. Put it in the bucket.

    – That was my father's.

    – No keepsakes, sir. You have to put it in the bucket.

    He sparks the stun-baton and the man pulls off his watch. In his pocket, Eli feels the photograph. He can't let them take it from him. Up ahead, a woman is being swept now. The guard pulls something from her hand— a rosary—but just laughs and gives it back.

    – That won't do you much good, here, Ma'am.

\#

Then it's Eli's turn; he's being beckoned forward, photo crumpled in his fist, hidden, he hopes. It's all he has left. He won't let them take it from him.

    – On you go, sir. Over there. Belt and shoes off.

    He walks over to the x-ray machine at the far left, past others where passengers are being prodded up onto the conveyor belts, made to lie down on their backs, bodies reduced to the status of luggage. He doesn't complain when it's his turn for the belt to take him into darkness, pause for a second, and then bring him out the other side. He's dragged to his feet, takes a step forward.

    – When I say.

    The guard uncaps a red marker, draws a strange sigil on his left shoulder, flicks his head.

    – *Now* you can go. Up the stairs, sir.

\#

Matthew's bare feet slap on cold stone steps and he clenches his teeth to stop them chattering, pulls the green sheet tighter round him, though it's more for decency than warmth, to cover him, to cover the sigil of his sin. He wants to throw up. He wants to scream and run, no matter what it means. He wants to crawl into a corner and die. But how can he die if he's already dead? Where can he run if this place is what he thinks it is? And all around him he can see how those who lose it are treated by the guards, the pitiless herding of the panicked, slipping on their own piss and shit, sobbing as they crawl on. The rank stench of human terror fills his nostrils.

He won't let himself go crazy, he thinks. It's not what it seems.

In the upper hall there are more people, more than a single ferry's worth, he's sure, divided out into a dozen lines stretching down to a row of desks at the far end, each staffed by a uniformed official. Beyond the desks, there are more uniforms, different styles but the same drab grey, guards on doors that open into darkness as the prisoners are dismissed from the desks, sent this way or that with a wave of a hand and a few short words. Over the sobs and whimpers, every so often, as he stands and waits or shuffles forward, he can hear an official's verdict, callous and abrupt.

A woman in a miniskirt.

– Adultery, this way.

A tramp in layered clothes so frayed you can't tell where one coat ends and another begins.

– Suicide, over there.

#

He's near the front of his own line when he spots the black guy standing quiet and studious, looking off to one side cool as can be, as the official checks his mark. Matthew follows his gaze to a door marked *No Entry*.

– Murder—

The place erupts as the man—jeez, but he's fast—grabs the official, hauls him out over the desk and slams his face into the floor. Then he's up and over the desk, stun-baton in hand, fighting his way towards the door, dodging batons, using his own, kicking and punching.

He nearly makes it. The first shock brings him to his knees, baton dropping from his grip, but he's up again immediately. Still, he's surrounded and—Matthew closes his eyes as the batons start to fall, but can't block out the cries and curses, the sounds of the struggle. The slam of a door.

– Your mark. Come on.

Matthew opens his eyes to find himself at the front of the line, an official leaning forward to pull the sheet from his shoulder, baring a sigil of two interlinked circles, each with an arrow coming off it, up and to the right. The guard sneers a smile of sorts.

– This isn't right, Matthew cuts off the man's words. You can't do this. He backs away, bumping past the person behind him in the queue.

– I've done nothing wrong, he says. Nothing.

He's still screaming his innocence as they drag him, bare feet sliding on the slick floor, sheet half-torn from his body, past the desk and towards a grey door, opening now into the blackness that swallows him.

#

Pale Grey Walls

He wakes in a room with pale grey walls, no windows other than the one in the door, and little in the way of furniture—just the bed he's lying in, a chair in one corner, bedside cabinet, blaring TV bracketed to the facing wall. A logo in the corner of the screen says Vox News, while a subtitle names the reporter as Trent Knightly. The man shouts over sirens and gunfire.

– grotesque or glorious, who can say? But make no mistake; here in the Village we're seeing scenes of carnage and chaos, of cannibalism and carnality, that have opened this reporter's eyes. It's a brutal bloodbath of butchery and….

#

Matthew scans the room for the remote but sees nothing. He slides out of the bed, finds a pair of slippers waiting for his feet, and pads around the room, searching. There's a robe hung on the back of the door, so he pulls it on, but there's no remote to be found. The set itself is just within reach but there's no buttons, no switches, and the power cable on the back is moulded to the unit, the other end disappearing into the wall; he tries to pull it, but it won't budge. Even the aerial won't disconnect.

On the screen as he steps back, police are shooting rioters. Men in fireproofs, helmets, and breathing gear sweep flamethrower jets into the shattered windows of shops. Paramedics strap screaming burn victims into straitjackets. All of them wear uniforms of grey.

– This isn't right.

#

Outside in the corridor, there are doctors, nurses, orderlies, more patients, all in grey, none paying him much attention. The sound of the TV isn't much quieter. It comes from every room he passes, from sets on walls at every corner. There's no escaping the damn things. Through a few open doors he sees other patients, some sitting on their beds, gazing blankly at the screen, some in chairs, staring at the wall, some huddled in corners, crying. He starts to walk faster, but there's no change to the corridors, no signs for exits, just a maze of wards and rec rooms. He starts to run.

#

He's not sure how long he's been running, walking, stopping to catch his breath now and then, running again, when he finally finds himself at a steel gate, on the other side of which a long corridor stops in a dead end and the only window he's seen in the whole place, small and white, a little square of frosted glass. He just stands there looking at it. He's still staring a while later when he feels a hand on his shoulder.

– Don't even think about it, kid, says a voice behind him.

#

Orders From Below

The man is ginger-haired, dressed in a gown and robe, another patient.

– I'm Red, he says.

– Matthew.

– You think that window means there's a way out, right? It doesn't.

Matthew's not sure he really wants an answer to the question on his mind. But he has to ask.

– What is this place?

– The Institute, says Red. We're here to be cured, you know.

Matthew smiles with relief.

– So I'm crazy? he says. This is a hospital. I'm crazy.

Red laughs.

– They might call you crazy. But I doubt that's why you're here. Wake up, kid. You've seen the TV. *This is Trent Knightly for Vox News, bringing you the hottest stories from the streets of Hell.*

#

– No. It can't be.

– No? Welcome to perdition, kid. The infernal city of the sinful dead.

– No. God—

– Wouldn't do this? Red says. Have you *read* the Bible? Trust me, this place is more wire and bromine than fire and brimstone, but it's damnation, not delusion. Guess you were a naughty boy.

Matthew looks back at the window. One glimpse

of daylight as an impossible dream, he thinks, and a thousand TVs as the never-ending nightmare.

– Infotainment 24/7, says Red, all the medication you never wanted, kid, you'll love it here, just *love* it. And talking of bread and circuses for the masses, it should be time for our daily crust. Come on.

#

They sit across from each other, at the canteen table, other patients and staff around them hunched over trays of slop. Matthew shovels gruel into his mouth and swallows, tries to chew it as little as possible, to *taste* it as little as possible. It doesn't work very well.

– It's the doctors that are the worst, says Red. The orderlies, they'll beat the crap out of you, but a punch in the face is just a punch in the face. The doctors want to get into your head. They're seriously fucking—

Red cuts himself off with a look over Matthew's shoulder, lowers his eyes to his food. Matthew glances back to see a doctor stalking down the aisle between the tables, interns in tow.

– …medication in the food, of course, he's saying, Rohypnol, Ritalin—

His smooth spiel stops in mid-flow as his pager beeps, his smile exchanged for a furrowed brow. One hand makes a *wait here* sign to the interns.

– A second.

#

He checks the number on the pager, clips it back on his belt, and digs a cellphone from his trouser pocket, walks away a distance. He talks quietly for a minute, then gives a *yes, sir*, snaps the cellphone shut.

– Orders from below, he says, sleek smile returning. As I was saying….

Matthew watches them walk on, looks down at the gloop in his tray. He pushes the crud away, but Red stops him with a hand on his forearm.

– Best if you eat it, he says. They don't like it if you *act out*. This place has lower levels, you understand?

– Lower levels, says Matthew numbly.

#

The Sound of Doors Closing

Seven stands in total darkness, listening to the sound of doors closing, locks turning, bolts slamming into place. The clink of his shackles as he twists in this cell no larger than a coffin. His own low growls through the gag that's in his mouth. He gave up slamming his shoulder against the steel walls a few hours ago, gave up kicking at the door some hours before that. At least, it felt like hours; he has no way to know. Now he just waits, held upright more by the walls than by his tired legs.

#

A thin shutter slides open to blinding light, and he blinks, narrows his eyes to slits. The guard's face is just a blur in the painful brightness.

– Welcome to Hell, Mister Seven, says a voice. I'm Johnson, and I'll be your demon this evening.

The shutter slides shut, and it's dark again.

A key turns in the lock.

#

The light when the door opens is even more glaring, too bright and too brief to see more than a glimpse—the orange jumpsuit he's wearing, the shackles holding his arms to his waist, guards in grey uniforms, a black hood in the hands of one—before the hood is thrown over his head, pulled tight. Seven feels his legs buckle, rough hands shoving him back and up. More locks are unclicked, and then he's being dragged forward by the arms, shuffling to try to find his feet.

– The famous Mister Seven, the guard says. Hear you've sent a lot of men our way, a *lot*. We have big plans for you, motherfucker. Oh, yeah, it's going to be fun to break you, Mister Seven. Eh, boys?

– More fun than kittens, boss, says a second voice.

– Kittens, yeah, I like that. Think that's what we'll call you: Mister Kitten. Our little bundle of fun.

#

Too weak to struggle, dragged along too fast, the only resistance Seven can offer is threats muffled by the gag, so he lets his anger cool into a calm resolve, like putting a TV on mute inside his head, a war movie transformed to silent images, distanced by the strange quietude of slaughter without sound. He focuses on the footsteps and the voices round him, separates them out… three guards by the sound of it.

– Boss, this kitten isn't even struggling.

– Pussy.

– Don't kid yourself. Mister Kitten's just waiting for his chance. Aren't you, motherfucker? But you've had all the fucking chances you're ever getting. Ever.

Seven feels their grips loosen as he's half-thrown and half-shoved ahead. He tumbles forward, hits concrete floor and rolls. He's still trying to twist his way up to his knees when he feels their grips return, hands round his ankles now as well as on each arm, lifting him.

– Kitten in a sack, boys. What we gonna do with him?

Then the laughter is killed by the splash of the plunge and the thrash of bubbles around his head, wet canvass clamping to his face, icy water pouring in his nose, being coughed out and snorted and sucked in as his lungs react in desperate rebellion and it's all he can do to fight the gasping, gulping panic of drowning.

#

New Meat

The hiss and gurgle of the shower wakes Belle gradually

to the feel of water trickling over her hair and face, lukewarm on her body. Cold tiles against her naked back. Curled up in a foetal ball, wall to her back, she's in the corner of a shower cubicle, curtain pulled aside to reveal the cracked tiles, stained enamel, and chipboard surfaces of a dingy bathroom. Hand on the wall to steady herself, she stands, turns the water off and—

—just makes it to the toilet bowl as a rush of memories—Johnny's fists and feet, the ferry and the guards—grips her by the gut and squeezes; she retches, coughs. Nothing comes and the dry heaves of fear pass. It was a bad trip; that's all it was. Johnny knocked her about a bit, so she got high, had a bad dream.

But the face that looks back at her from the mirror is unbruised, like the beating never happened, and lying on the counter beside the sink, she sees as she splashes water on that face, is a miniature soap with a custom label for a hotel. Hotel California.

#

The room is trashy in all ways—stained sheets on the unmade bed, peeling wallpaper, dirty red carpet, and tatty red curtains that open on a bricked-up window. There's a *Crying Boy* print above the headboard, a wood-panelled TV in a corner of the room, a standard lamp, the basics. The clothes in the closet are equally trashy, but no worse than what Johnny makes her wear, so she pulls on a pair of tight denims and a leopard-print top. She's not sure what she's doing, but she knows she needs to get out of here, keep moving. If she keeps moving she doesn't have to think about where she is. She slips a pair of red heels on, pulls on a fake fur coat over the top of it all and heads for the door. It's locked, and, unlike any hotel room she's ever seen, the boxy lock with the keycard slot is on the inside. She starts looking through the drawers in the bedside cabinet, finds her rosary and a remote for the TV but nothing else. She goes through the pockets of the clothes in the closet. Still nothing. After a while, she gives up, sits down on the edge of the bed.

#

She's still frozen there fuck knows how much later, rosary in one hand, remote in the other, watching the horrors of Hell on the TV screen, when the lock on the door clicks.

Even without the TV imagery of cops shooting "rioters," beating "looters," she'd know just from the look on his face that the man in the grey cop uniform is not here to save her. She knows the leer of a bad john, those who want much more than sex, who want games of pain and humiliation, who hurt you bad and walk out without paying. She looks at the handcuffs and the stun-baton on his belt.

– So you're settling in, he says. Belle, isn't it? Don't get up.

He closes the door, takes his coat off and hangs it on the knob. The hat follows.

– You've worked it out? he says. You won't gimme some whiny *this ain't happening* shit, right? You know you're fucked, and you're going to be fucked for a very long time. Right?

– Who are you? she says.

– You can call me Officer Gordon if you want, he says, but I'd like it if you called me Daddy.

#

He's draping his pants on the chair when the radio on his belt crackles into life, a call.

– Fuck. You, take your clothes off. Get into bed.

Belt draped over his shoulder, radio unclipped, he wanders into the bathroom, shoves the door half-closed.

– Yeah, Gordon here, he says. What's up? Sure,

sure. Orders from below. Whatever. Can it wait?

The only answer Belle makes out is static hiss. She creeps over to his jacket, takes it off the hook, slips a hand into each pocket one by one. There's a small metal case, a matchbook, but no keycard. Belle listens to the trickle of piss in the toilet bowl, a sigh of relief. She looks at the pants, treads softly over to them.

– Good, he's saying. 'Cause, you wouldn't believe how sweet the new meat is. Tell the boys they'll enjoy their cut of this one, I swear.

The toilet flushes just as she finds the keycard in his back pocket, slips it out. More speed than quiet now, she crosses to the door, turning the card to find the stripe, swipe it through the lock. The handle *clicks*. She's halfway through the door when he hauls her back by the hair, grabbing the keycard from her hand, shoving her onto the bed.

– I thought you were smarter, he says. Bitch, where you think you're going? This is all there is for you now. Forever.

He twirls the keycard through his fingers like a gambler playing with a chip.

– You know, you're lucky, he says. Some don't get it this good.

The door swings closed behind him with a click.

\#

A Murder of Children

The slam of a car door snaps Eli awake, eyes open. He's curled up in damp trash and oily puddles beside a dumpster, looking past it, down a back alley, at black boots and a grey uniform, a cop stepping down out of a black-and-white parked across the entry, thumping his own door closed as he looks over the hood, nods to his partner. Both of them have snub submachine guns in their right hands, what look like camcorders in their left. Viewscreens flipped out, they scan the alley. Night vision? Eli wriggles himself behind the dumpster, out of their line of sight; he doesn't know why he does it, just that something in the way they carry themselves, something slow and cold, robotic or reptilian, says *threat*. He twists himself upright, huddles his back into a nook of shadow where the dumpster meets brick wall, sits out from it a little.

Only then does Eli notice the man pressed back into the darkness of the facing doorway, the matted beard, the filthy finger held up to his lips.

– You hear that? says one of the cops.

– Could be rats.

– Could be. Looks like Forgotten territory though. Smells like it too. You seeing anything?

– Nada.

– Well, let's sweep the rats out if they're in there.

#

Garbage crumps and water splashes underfoot, and Eli huddles further back, tries to squeeze himself behind the dumpster. The first cop is just coming into sight when, further down the alley, there's a sudden flurry of rags and newspaper, a third vagrant tumbling from behind a cardboard box, bolting.

– There!

The burst of gunfire jolts stark terror into Eli, shuddering his nerves even as it batters the vagrant like a puppet danced on strings. Drops him. The cop in front walks up to the dead man, camcorder lowered at his side. He turns back to grin at his partner, strolling up now past the dumpster's edge.

– Told you I heard something.

Across from Eli, the other vagrant steps out from his hiding place, foot lifted over trash, lowered without a sound. He steps out straight into the first cop's line of sight, right at the second's shoulder. Eli watches in horror, biting back a cry, but the cops don't seem to even notice. The first cop stares straight at him, through him, like he isn't even there, or at least does so until… he brings the camcorder back up.

– Shit!

He brings the gun up.

– Out of the way!

Comes running back.

– The fucker's right behind you!

Fires.

#

– All clear?

– No more down this end, far as I can see.

– OK, let's roll. It's getting fucking cold. And Gordon says there's new meat at the California. Fresh off the boat.

Eli huddles in behind the dumpster, waiting till long after he's sure the cops have left the alley before sliding out. The dead vagrants lie where they were shot, the corpses left to rot, just two more piles of garbage in the dereliction of the alley. Eli crouches down to roll one over onto his back, to run rough fingers over a face ruined by drink, the blotchy, pitted skin of an alcoholic. He wipes blood from the slack mouth, closes the blindly staring eyes, but there's no dignity in the wreck of a human being. If there's no dignity in life, thinks Eli, why would there be dignity in death, in Hell?

He stands, looks around at this alley, this urban valley of the shadow of death, thinks of the grand claims of a psalm that once gave him solace. *I will fear no evil, for thou art with me. Thy rod and thy staff....*

In the pocket of his coat, a crumpled photograph is the nearest he has to such comfort now.

#

Out on the street, beyond the alley, it's a brownstone city of gun shops and clip joints, pawn shops and credit companies. He watches nervously for cop cars on the road, sees only taxis with blood-spattered windows, glimpses of grotesquery inside, pressed to the glass, slavering. He weaves his way through a fight of youths, a murder of children round a burning pram, a harangue of businessmen fighting over a corpse. People shove past, bumping shoulders, stumbling, but they just regain their footing and walk on, only the slightest flickers of confusion on their faces, dissipating in an instant. He mumbles at one woman, grabs her sleeve, but it's like she just can't hold him in her consciousness.

Outside a video equipment shop, he watches his image in a TV screen, only the mechanical eye of the camera in the window seeming to admit of his existence. On the sidewalk underfoot, marking the spot dead centre of the camera's frame, someone has scrawled a sigil in chalk. It's a sign he recognises from a past life of lectures and tutorials, books on sociology and history, books he read and books he wrote—a hobo sign. It means *danger*. Beside it there's a second sign, one he hopes he's reading right as he sets off in the direction pointed by the arrow under it.

He's not invisible, he thinks. It's just… nobody pays him any mind. Just like nobody notices the vagrants lying dead on the sidewalks, in the gutters and doorways, bloated green or burnt to black, every hundred yards or so as he trudges the long blocks of the city of the damned, following the trail of hobo signs that leads him to the derelict brownstone, to the door that opens into a hallway of eggshell-yellow walls and filthy floorboards, to another door, the sigil spray-painted upon it. From behind the door comes a tumult of voices, scents of food.

The door opens to his push and Eli walks into a hall of wretches, Hell's soup kitchen. A woman in a ratty Salvation Army uniform takes him by the sleeve, pulls him inside and asks his name, but all he can think of is the promise written in the hobo sign.

– Shelter, he says. Is this shelter?

#

Sweet Dreams

– Now, Belle, says Gordon. Don't cry.

He lays the half-finished carton of noodles on the bedside cabinet, unlocks the handcuffs holding her wrist to the bed frame and hooks them back on his belt. His voice offers the cold comfort of a million pimps.

– You've got a roof over your head, he says, food in your stomach. It's not so bad. You don't know what it's like out on the street, how few even make it through their first day. But it doesn't have to be like that. We can keep you going for a *real* long time. You treat me good and I'll take care of you.

She flinches from the hand that brushes hair out of her face.

– You don't believe me, Belle, don't trust me?

He pulls his jacket on and reaches into a pocket, pulls out the metal case she noticed earlier, tosses it onto the bed.

– A token of good faith, he says.

As he slides the keycard though the lock on the door, she picks the case up, opens it.

– Sweet dreams, he says before pulling the door shut.

She listens to his footsteps fade, stares at the contents of the case: a little bag of brown powder; a spoon; a syringe.

#

Eli takes a seat at one of the tables, bowl of broth cradled in his hands. *We're the lucky ones*, the woman in the uniform had said. *It's not so bad being Forgotten, long as you stay away from the cameras. Long as nobody members you.*

Around him, these *Forgotten* hunch over their bowls, or lie curled in blankets, sleeping bags, or overcoats, on beds of cardboard matting, wooden pallets. The few who meet his eyes gaze back at him bleakly.

– You must be just off the boat, right? I can tell. It's the edgy look.

A teenage boy, pale and skinny, dressed in an old army jacket, slides into the seat across from him.

– So how'd *you* buy this trip, he says. Shotgun? Overdose? Short step off a subway platform?

– Something like that, says Eli.

– You don't want to talk about it? That's cool, man.

He pulls a cigarette from behind his ear and lights it, leaning forward, manner sliding from casual to confidential.

– So you holding? Junk, pills, booze, whatever? Only, these Damnation Army fruitcakes, they don't dig that, act like they care but, fuck, they just think playing saints in Hell might get them time off for good behaviour. They find out you're holding, then you're outta here, you dig? You can give it to me though, if you want. I know hiding places. I can keep it safe for you.

A snort of derision from an old woman along the table earns a scowl from the boy.

– I don't have anything, says Eli.

The boy's eyes narrow in scrutiny, smile holding for a second before curling to disdain as he scrapes back his chair.

– Fucking waste of time.

The boy stalks away, and the old woman looks up from her bowl.

– The little junky talks shit, she says, but he's right about one thing. No one gives a fuck about you. No more than they did in life. No more than *you* did. That's *our* Hell.

Eli bows his head. There was a time he would have said grace for this thin slop and wretched shelter, for any charity whether born of altruism or self-interest. Not now. He says nothing.

#

– Shut up, says Matthew quietly. Shut up, shut up, shut up.

On the TV, Trent Knightly carries on regardless, shouting over the noise of rotor blades, the image on the screen an aerial shot of a smouldering building. The camera zooms in on blackened, bloodied people staggering through ruins.

– Yes, the desperate hunt for survivors and salvage goes on, but it all seems futile now, Carson, futile and foolish, a vain attempt. Surely, there's little hope of— wait! Wait! I think I see something. There's something happening. Yes, there's a rabble in the rubble, Carson, closing in—looks like they've found someone.

Propped up with pillows at his back, Matthew draws his knees up to his chin, buries his face in folded forearms.

– Yes, it's a woman, Carson, and they're going wild for her. I don't know how well you can see this, but it's a terrible sight, Carson, a truly awful vision of savage lust.

– Shut up, says Matthew. Shut up. Shut—

A call from the hallway cuts him off.

– Lights out!

The plunge into silence and darkness is a relief so blessed his throat tightens to a swallow, tightens again, then releases into gulping sobs he can't control.

#

The dark is stripped away by white light, burning bright even through his closed eyes. A shriek of guitar feedback, crashing drums, a sheer cacophony of formless beats and riffs and guttural vocals warped to roars blasts Seven from his half-sleep. Hell's own raging metal fills his ears, his head, his bones, and Seven struggles to control the frustration rising in him. Fists clenched to white knuckles, teeth gritted, every muscle in his body tensed, he tries to ride his anger, rein it in with steel resolve. Breath in. Breath out. It's only noise and light, only pain and exhaustion. It won't last. It'll stop again.

It could be five minutes later, or fifteen or fifty, when his control finally breaks and he explodes into a wildcat thrashing, his gagged screams inaudible even to himself.

It could be five minutes later, or fifteen or fifty, when the music and light shut down as suddenly as they started, peace blanketing his aching body and blurred mind in the comfort, the bliss, of the quiet and the dark.

It could be five minutes later, or fifteen or fifty, when it starts all over again.

#

Awakening in Hell

Eli blinks, head jerking up, left and right. Confusion rules: noise; people; cameras; lighting; a microphone with a plastic logo that says Vox News, shoved into his face. He pulls his pile of blankets up, shuffles back against the wall.

– That's perfect. That's the fear we want.

A reporter with a jutting chin and wide grin points a camera at him, studies him in the viewscreen.

– Start with a close-up head-shot on this rat, he says. Then on to me.

A stylist fluffs the man's coiffure as a cameraman

counts down with his fingers—*three, two, one*—and points.

– Society's invisibles! Eternity's untouchables! Hell's Forgotten! And this sorry spectacle of a man is only one sad story among thousands. Yes, I'm Trent Knightly and today we're here in a Damnation Army shelter, where the dregs, the debris, the detritus of Hell's shades cower in destitution, craving only the cold comfort of a bowl of soup and a bed for the night. Today we're delving, diving, into the lives and deaths of these Forgotten failures, their souls squandered in suicide, surrendered to despair. What is it like to seek the mercy of death and find the misery of Hell? Tell us your story, friend. Tell us what brought you to this awful end.

The reporter crouches, pulls a corner of blanket down to reveal Eli's photograph of his family. He beckons the cameraman: *Shoot this*.

#

– A story of lost love, broken dreams of happy families, is that it?

– Leave that alone.

Eli snatches the photo up, shoves the reporter back, and rounds on the cameraman as he hauls himself to his feet.

– Get the hell away from me. All of you.

The reporter recovers quickly, rolling to his feet. He signals behind him, turns back to the cameraman.

– And so we see the danger of the desperate, the ferocious resentment rising among the Forgotten, an irrational rage ready to erupt at any point. Yes, I can feel the tension in the air, the lurking menace of the rats among us, the menace we call *riot*.

It's only then that Eli notices the guards beyond the camera crew, sweeping through the shelter, herding vagrants into clusters at the barrels of their guns.

Not *riot*, he thinks.

Massacre.

#

The rec room is empty but for Red, sitting in the front row of the plastic chairs that fan out round the TV, Matthew in the row behind. On-screen, statistics scroll under a caption that reads "Hell's Forgotten Threat?" In centre frame, Knightly is shouting over gunfire again, praising the virtues of his crew's *embedded troops, their valour in the face of violent vengeance, in the face of madmen driven to destruction by despair and desolation*. Dressed in grey camouflage combats, wearing night-vision goggles, armed with M-16s, those embedded troops seem to be slaughtering the residents of a homeless shelter.

The camera catches a whirl of frayed coats, a vagrant rolling out from under a table behind the troops, hitting his feet in a dead run. Bullets splinter the frame but the man skids and slides, dives through a doorway as gunfire pounds plaster walls to dust around him.

– Bastard, says Red. Trent bloody Knightly.

He looks back at Matthew, over his shoulder.

– I used to be Forgotten, he says, until that bastard membered me on bloody prime time. Thought I had it bad before but….

He shakes his head.

#

Watching the massacre, Matthew gleans only the vaguest gist of Red's rant, that Hell has an underclass that scrapes by on the streets, that it's a better existence than the Institute.

– You ever try to leave? he asks.

Red holds up an arm, pulls the sleeve back to reveal a bandaged wrist.

– Every day, he says. The only way there is.

Matthew lowers his voice as he leans in towards Red.

– How can you die when you're already dead? he says.

– Take a look up there, says Red. It's pretty easy. Heads up.

He nods at the doctor striding into the rec room, orderlies in tow, file open in his hands.

– Matthew? says the doctor. I'm Doctor Meikler. Come with me.

– What for? What's going on?

– It's time for your treatment to begin. Your cure.

#

A Small Ball of Coiled Anger

Belle sits on the edge of the bed, panties on, rosary in hand, lit cigarette in her mouth. Gordon lies on top of the covers behind her, naked; she feels her skin crawl as his hand drifts down her spine, but doesn't flinch.

– So was it as good as the first time? he says. Not yesterday, I mean, with me. The *first* time. First time you ever let a man touch you, do things to you, even though you knew it was wrong?

– I don't remember, she says.

She takes a draw on the cigarette.

– Sure you do, he says. I bet you remember clear as day.

He pushes himself upright, shuffles round to sit beside her, one hand sliding to the back of her neck, the other taking the cigarette out of her fingers. He takes a draw on it.

– You never forget your first time, pumpkin. Daddy coming into your room one night… or maybe it was Uncle Bob, or Mr Peterson next door? Someone you trusted getting just a little bit closer than was right, running his fingers through your hair, like this, saying

37

how smooth your shoulder was, right here, how pretty you were, how soft, saying not to worry, hush now, this'll be our little secret.

He takes another draw, lets the smoke drift from his open leer of a grin.

– Was it as good as that? he says.

#

– You're a sick bastard, she says.

He takes her wrist, pulls her arm across his lap to stroke the inside of the forearm, lingering at the track marks.

– Suffering corrupts, he says. But you know that, don't you? There's no dignity in suffering. It just grinds you down until you're just another little junky whore.

– Or a sadistic prick. What's *your* story, asshole? Who was *your* first? Did Daddy teach you how to be a twisted fuck?

Gordon takes another draw on the cigarette, holds it, then blows a billow of smoke. And jabs the lit cigarette into her arm. He laughs at her yelp of pain, her curses.

– Want me to kiss it better, baby?

In the bathroom, as she runs cold water over it, she looks at herself in the mirror, hating what she sees.

#

When the splash finally comes, followed by the trickle of water from the sodden hood, the splutters of his coughs, Seven is too busy with his lungs' attempts to get air into them to care about the hands lifting him up, dragging him back to his cell. He's too fucked to be more than a passive victim, retching, coughing water out through his nostrils, shaking his head to loosen the hood, get air in. He's too physically wrecked to focus on their taunts and jeers as they latch him back up to his chains, pull the hood from his head, and slam the door of his cell closed once again.

#

But there's just enough of a small ball of coiled anger in his chest that when the slot slides open and the guard leans forward to spit in his face he looks up to meet the man's eyes with the unblinking threat of a vicious dog that knows only one word: *kill*. The slot slides closed.

– Later, says the guard.

Seven turns the word over in his head. Yes. Later.

#

Aversion Therapy

– If you don't co-operate, Matthew, then we can't help you. And we all want to help you.

Meikler's flourish encompasses the circle of patients in plastic chairs, all with their eyes on Matthew… who looks back at them with sullen hostility. The group therapy room is unfurnished but for the chairs and a flip-chart, a few inspirational posters: *Acceptance is the first step to true penitence*; *From sin comes shame, from shame salvation*.

– So, I'll ask you again, says Meikler. What is it about you that God despises? Why does He hate you?

– I don't know, says Matthew. I don't know why I'm here.

– I think you do. I've read your file, Matthew. I know your secrets.

– You tell me, then. Why am I here?

– We need to hear it from you, Matthew. You need to face up to your own condition, or….

– Or what? says Matthew, rising. What?

#

The leather strap bites into his wrist as Doctor Meikler tightens it.

– Leave me alone. Let me go.

Matthew pushes his shoulder against the weight of the orderly buckling the strap across his chest. A thick forearm slams him back into the padding of a chair straight out of a nightmare of dentist torturers.

– Please. You don't have to do this.

A sharp tug on the strap across his forehead pulls his head back into the rubber vice. His heart pounds, panic rising. It's not just the chair that scares him. It's the machine with the wires.

#

– Don't you want to be cured, Matthew?

He hears the tearing of tape, feels electrodes press to his temples.

– If you cure me then you'll let me go, he says. Right? I just want out of here. Please… just… you don't have to do this.

Meikler sighs as the orderly prises Matthew's jaw open, forces a bit between his teeth.

– Out of here, Matthew? There is no *out of here*. But if we cure you… you might be a valuable member of our staff, Matthew. One day.

He wheels a little TV–DVD combo set on a trolley up in front of the chair, clicks it on to a movie of writhing flesh, bad music, and voices moaning. Matthew squeezes his eyes shut at the sight. It's sick, sinful. It's not him.

#

– Aversion therapy, says Meikler. I was like you once, you know; many of us were. All those impure thoughts. Not now. You understand? Once we've cured you, you'll be *proud* to do for others what we did for you. Open your eyes and look at the screen, Matthew.

Through the bit, Matthew whimpers pleading tones—a whine that becomes a scream as the voltage wracks his body with arching, tensing, juddering pain. It's a while before he understands the words being spoken quietly in his ear.

– Let's try that again, shall we? Open your eyes and

look at the screen.

Then the pain comes again.

\#

A Montage of Suffering

And it goes on, eternity breaking sense apart to a montage of suffering.

This is Hell: a man in a jumpsuit and chains, in a steel coffin too small to collapse in; dark silence broken by deafening noise, blinding light; the stink of his own urine and shit; draggings and drownings; beatings; being stripped to nothing but a hood; exhaustion; starvation; tubes forced down his throat, to feed him or to distend his belly with more water than it was ever meant to hold; a burning rage against the endless humiliation, against the helplessness.

\#

This is Hell: a man alone on the streets, eating garbage to survive; seeking shelter with the Forgotten; following their signs from safe haven to safe haven; talking to ghosts in the shadows; bartering knowledge for food; being betrayed, beaten, and thrown from shelters as one of *them*, not Forgotten now but *membered*; fleeing citizens who see him, recoil in disgust, hurl bottles and bricks, set upon him with savage fear, the TV face of a Forgotten mass that he's no longer even one of; hiding from cops who stalk the night, intent on eradicating these vagrant vermin who, in their utter dereliction, deserve only oblivion.

\#

This is Hell: a woman in a hotel room with no way out, her only visitors her pimp cop and the stream of johns he sends to her every day; naked on the bed, handcuffed to the posts, while they fuck her; living on scraps of take-out; fingering food into her mouth as she watches endless death on the box, wonders what torments you go to if you die in Hell, or if it's just oblivion; buying junk dreams with her own degradation; wanting to store up enough for an overdose but lacking the will or the nerve, or both; wrapping her rosary round her arm, winding it tight to raise a vein; puking with the shakes after a day or two in solitude; pounding on the door of her room, pounding until she slumps against it, crumples into a ball.

#

This is Hell: a kid shouting his denial against the baying circle of patients and the doctor who leads the ceremony of shame; screaming his pain and horror as the voltage burns through his brain; keeping his eyes squeezed shut from the deeper horror in abject admission of his sin; sitting in his room, throwing a chair at the brutality on TV, watching it bounce off as the reporter grins with vulture relish.

– This is the Knightly Report on Vox News, bringing you the hard truths you don't want to hear.

The door opens, and Matthew gazes hollowly at Red, standing in the doorway, wearing his new orderly's uniform. Matthew can't recall how long it is since the nearest he had to company here was broken, turned into a trustee.

– Lights out, says the demon who was once, like him, a human being.

ACT TWO—FLIGHT

A Show of Drowning

As his head plunges into the water, Seven holds his breath, starts counting, *one to ten*. He's had plenty of time to practice holding his breath, can take the near-drownings just a little bit better than the guards realise. *Eleven to twenty*. He's had plenty of time to observe his own reactions on the verge of drowning, practice faking the convulsions and collapse before they actually kick in. *Twenty-one to thirty*. Plenty of time to adjust to broken sleep. *Thirty-one to forty*. Learn to use his chains and the confines of the cell as counterforce to his exercise. *Forty-one to fifty*. Learn to cut his mind off from unbearable sensation. *Fifty-one to sixty*.

He's had plenty of time to plan.

Another half a minute.

He's pushed himself beyond the limit of endurance just to see what they would do to revive him.

Just a few seconds more.

Now he gives them a show of drowning—shudders, shakes, and sudden stillness—like they've never seen.

#

His body flops to the floor, head smacking concrete, a dead weight.

– Fuck. He's not breathing.

– Shit! Not again.

Seven feels the hood dragged from his head, the gag torn off to free his airway for the CPR, but his eyes stay glazed, a dead man's stare, until one guard bends down to haul him up into a Heimlich hold. Then: His head slams back into the fucker's nose; he kicks himself into a backward roll over the stunned man; scythes his legs to sweep the second bastard's feet from under him; twists, slips a crook of shackled arm around the first guard's head, and *wrenches*; rolls, kicks out with both feet; hits the second guard's chin with his heels, snapping it back; he rolls again, out of the path of the third guard's swinging stun-baton sparking on the wet floor; kung fu flips himself to his feet; turns as the last man lunges; hits him with a dropkick in the chest that sends him staggering back, over the edge of the bath where the fuckers have been drowning Seven every day for what seems like an eternity.

On his back on the floor, he enjoys the crackle and thrash of the third guard being juiced by his own stun-baton in the water.

Now, he thinks. Keys.

#

Seven slams the guard face-first into the steel door, sound resounding down the corridor of cell after cell, like some bastard hybrid of solitary confinement and a school locker room. Looks like it goes straight on forever, but Seven knows that if you walk far enough in one direction you end up back where you started, crazy as that is. He wrenches the man's unbroken left arm further up his back now, pounds his face into the metal again, reaches down to punch a shattered femur. The guard shrieks. Seven pulls the pistol from the motherfucker's holster, jams it in his own belt, pats down the man's pockets.

– How do I get out?

The guard splutters blood and broken teeth. Seven found him near the water-torture room, on his third circuit of a straight corridor. Fucker must have come from somewhere.

– You can't. The cells are hard-locks, but the wings, the whole level… this is high security. Psychometric corridors. You can find the exit if you know where to look but there's biometric locks.

– What biometrics?

He pushes the arm up higher, to the snap of cartilage.

– Thumbprints! Retina scans!

Seven swings the man round and against the door again, cocks the pistol at his forehead.

– OK, he says. So I'm going to need your thumbs and your eyes. Lead on.

#

The lock beeps, red light switching to green for *Go*. Seven shoulders the door into the stairwell open, throws the body through, and shoots the guard who catches it, two more coming down the stairs. The alarm is wailing but it's no more than a nuisance to Seven, signifies their panic, not his. He strips the shotgun and flak jacket from one dead guard, pulls the jacket on as he heads for the stairs down and—a stencil on the wall pulls him up short: Sublevel 16. Underground, he thinks. Sixteen floors.

Motherfucker.

He takes the stairs two at a time, neck craning, shotgun aimed at each landing as it comes in sight. Two more guards appear, and he drops to a knee, blasts them, takes out a third with the pistol in his left hand. Waits a second. No more. He moves on.

He's at the doorway to the thirteenth floor when the bullets pound the wall beside him, send him ducking back, firing the shotgun at a half dozen guards on the stairs above. Fuck. He fires a few shots with the pistol to hold them back while he reloads the shotgun. Leans out to send another blast their way. Jams the pistol in his belt and pulls out the package of bloody cloth stuffed in his open shirt. A severed thumb for pressing to the scanner. A gouged-out eye to hold up to the camera. Pistol in his hand again, he fires at the bastards above as the lock beeps.

He slams backwards through the door, into a corridor filled with the sound of TVs and the smell of disinfectant. A woman in a grey hospital gown and robe, wild-haired, wild-eyed, shuffles down the corridor towards him.

– Kill me, she says. Kill me.

– What the fuck? says Seven quietly.

#

The Lord of Hell

– Yes, I've been watching. It's quite entertaining.

The archangel sits, cellphone at his ear, eyes on the wall of screens—the trail of bodies down in Sublevel Sixteen, through the stairwell, the screen that shows the hitman even now putting a bullet in the head of some sad psych ward inmate.

– No, no lockdown. Let our rat run the maze, see what he does when he's cornered. Don't make it *too* easy for him, though. I *do* want him cornered. Once he realises he can't shoot his way out, he'll take a hostage, a human shield. All I want you to do is close off every other option.

He leans back in his leather chair, feet on the desk beside a small sphere, glowing golden-white like sunlight itself is trapped within. Which isn't too far from the truth.

– Call in more men then, says the Lord of Hell. Tell them it's orders from below.

#

Belle ignores the cop's face leering over her, grunting in time to his thrusts. She gazes at the ceiling, imagines it as a map of some distant country, cracks as rivers weaving and branching through deserts of tobacco stains, forests and mountains of damp and mould. This trick is plain vanilla, at least, compared to Gordon. All this guy wants is a quick hard wordless fuck, no sick fetishes or fantasies. If anything, his kink is for her to lie there, no response, an empty vessel of a being. It doesn't stop her hating him as much as all the others. He's probably the most fucked-up of them all. He's probably just pretending she's a corpse.

His radio spits static and a call sign as he's building up to orgasm—*Units twelve through twenty-one report.* He curses, keeps on thrusting through the second call, the third.

– …report. Over.

– Fuck!

He pulls out of her, cursing as he stalks to the radio, yammers into it in cop-speak codes. After, he hooks the radio back in its place, punches the wall.

– Fuck! Well, no meat for me, no treats for you. Some crazy's trying to shoot his way out of the Institute, and who gets called in to bring him down? High security, my ass. Third fucking breakout this year. Three escapes in four months. Shit, I stink of cheap whore.

He gathers his clothes and dumps them on the bed, stalks through to the bathroom. She hears the squeak of the shower knob, the spurting spray of water.

Three escapes, thinks Belle. Wonder if any of them made it.

#

– Warden, says the archangel, your men are street thugs in a uniform; they're expendable. But if our Mister Seven's alive at the end of this… oh, he'll be a wonderful demon once he's broken, *invaluable*. So when he takes his hostage you pull back, let him think he has leverage.

The archangel swings his feet off the desk, leans forward to pick up the sphere of radiance, turn it in his hand.

– Then we give the doggy a long leash, watch him run

full tilt at the gate, and break his own neck as that leash snaps tight. You let him see the door, the daylight… and then you shoot the hostage. And get Knightly in there. I want this televised.

He lays the sphere back on the desk, spins it.

– No, it'll take more than that to break this soul. But it's a start. And they *all* break in the end. OK?

He clicks the cellphone shut, lays it down on the desk and leans in towards the sphere of light.

– Yes, they all break in the end, he says. Don't they, old friend?

\#

In the bathroom, over the shower's patter, Belle's trick is still ranting.

– Fucking justice system pussies couldn't hold their own dick if you wrapped their fist around it.

Belle sits on the bed beside his clothes, thinking of the keycard in one of the pockets, of escape. The door to the bathroom is wide open, though; even if she could grab the keycard… could she make it without him seeing?

– That's if you could fucking *find* their dicks. I tell you….

His empty holster lies on top of his shirt. The tricks don't bring their weapons in with them. Wouldn't do for some *cheap whore* to blow their balls off while they snoozed after a hard day's play. She grabs a smoke from the pack on the bedside cabinet, twists a match out of the book in the ashtray. Fucking TV is all she'll ever see of the outside world.

– …wonder these ass-wipes don't fry themselves with their own sticks.

Belle strikes the match and lights the cigarette. She's stuck in this fucking room forever, looking at the same stinking bed, the same shitty curtains, the same ugly lamp....

She shakes the flame out, lays the cigarette down on the ashtray's edge. The noise of the shower stops as she stands, walks over to the lamp. As she runs a hand round the glass uplighter shade, she hears the slap of his wet feet on the bathroom floor. She hefts the lamp. It's not that heavy. Gives the cord a flick. Not that long.

But long enough.

– What the fuck was that?

The smash of the glass shade against the doorframe makes him drop the towel from his hair and turn. She swings the lamp again and takes out the bulb this time.

– What the fuck are you—? is all he has time to say before she jabs it into his balls like a fucking cattle-prod.

She slams the door shut as the spasming fucker hits the floor, drags the chair across the room and wedges its back under the handle. Fumbles frantically through his clothes and finds the keycard.

Fuck, she'll never make it. She knows that. But it's worth a try.

#

A Very Bad Man

– That's right, Carson. Sources in the Institute are saying there's *another* escape attempt in progress, a crazed killer on the loose. Will we see another bloodbath like before, brave officers gunned down like dogs in the line of duty? More lives lost in the rampage of a madman? I can't answer these questions yet, Carson, but we're headed to the scene right now, and I can promise we'll have the pictures for you soon, right here on Vox News.

Matthew tunes out the histrionic babble, focused on the panicked sounds outside his room as he eases the door open, pokes his head through. Meikler runs past, slapping off the reaching hands and questions of alarmed patients. He pushes through a set of swing doors, returns a second later with two men in flak jackets, pointing them back past Matthew's room. From that direction there's a gunshot, screams, then doors smack back against the wall. A surge of patients and staff sweeps through, a wave that—with another, closer gunshot—picks up the stragglers here and carries them past Matthew, past Meikler, and past the two guards now moving forward, guns at the ready, jogging up to the door to crouch, backs against the wall. One holds a little mirror on a stick up to the glass panel in one door, signals. They push through the doors together and—

#

An almighty boom sends two faceless bodies flying back through. The doors swing back, kick open again as a man strides through, shotgun in each hand. One swivels to aim on Matthew, the other points straight ahead.

– OK, who else wants to die? he says.

The thump of his body hitting the floor is Meikler's answer. Hands up, Matthew shakes his head—*no, sir*. The man shrugs, crouches to strip ammo from the dead guards, turns his head for a second like he's heard a sound, and—

– Wait. I know you, says Matthew. The ferry….

The man looks at him blankly, shrugs.

– I'll write you a postcard from the outside, he says.

He walks off down the corridor without a second glance at Matthew, who watches the doors swing shut, listens to the gunfire that follows. After a few seconds of staring dumbly at Meikler, out cold on the floor, he grabs the doctor's feet, drags him into his room.

#

Corners and corridors, the place is a fucking rabbit warren, wings of wards filled with the sound of TV and tantrums, loonies everywhere, and the guards blocking his way with tear gas and force of numbers, forcing him to backtrack. Seven's been lucky; he's still alive. But if there's a way out, that luck's not helping him find it. He could swear he's retraced his steps and ended up somewhere he's never been.

He leans out at a T-junction to check each way. Nothing left. Nothing right. A hand on his shoulder has him spinning, shotgun in the face of a young guy in a grey lab coat and a suit that are both a size too big.

– Wait! says the kid. It's me!

– What do you want?

– Same as you, he says. Out. And I know the way.

Seven studies the kid. He doesn't look quite as bugfuck as some of the crazies Seven has seen here. And if he knows this fucking maze…. He nods.

– One thing, says the kid. Can I borrow that? Just for a second.

He points at the pistol tucked into Seven's belt. Seven cocks his head, brings his shotgun to bear on the kid, just to be safe, as he hands him the gun. The kid trains it on a TV set perched on the wall facing them, where some tedious maggot is yammering about landing on the roof, having pictures of the carnage any minute. The kid pulls the trigger, and the screen explodes. He hands back the gun.

– OK, whitebread, says Seven. Lead on.

Corners and corridors, the boy leads him through the maze, heading back the way they came, and Seven follows.

#

Seven peers round the corner at the sandbags and armed guards blocking his way. Behind him, the kid, still in his doctor's drab, crouches over one of the many bodies left in Seven's wake, as much confusion on his face as anything.

– I don't get it, says Matthew. How can you die if you're already dead?

Seven looks at the guards hunkered down at the junction. At least a dozen of them. He gives the kid a cold eye.

– If it's got a mouth to ask stupid questions, he says, then I can blow its motherfucking head off, dig? Now. You're sure this is the only way?

– Yep. Maybe if there were more of us, the other patients….

Seven snorts.

– An army of basket cases? Get real, kid. I'm not here to lead a bunch of nut-jobs to salvation. Fuck, if this is Hell, they must be bad people anyway, right? Motherfuckers belong here.

– Nobody belongs here, says the kid.

– I do, says Seven. I am a *very* bad man. Sorry, kid.

And with that Seven hauls the kid up and shoves him out into the corridor, both shotguns pointed at his head.

– OK! he shouts. Listen up, motherfuckers! You fall back and let us through, or the good doctor gets a transfer to the morgue. *Comprendez?*

#

Broken Bulbs and Bare Wall

The guards pulled back out of their path, they move on, Seven following the kid, Matthew muttering sullenly, taking turns that… don't add up. They just made four right turns in a row, Seven is sure, should be back where they started, but it's like the corridors are shifting around them.

– You sure you know where this exit is? he says.

– I've been here a lot, says the kid.

He turns another right.

—This is it.

A barred gate closes off a dead-end corridor, a small white panel of light like a frosted window in the end wall. As the boy stands gazing at it in awe, Seven leans back against a door marked *STORAGE*.

– That's your way out? he says.

– It's a window. I don't know what floor we're on, but…. It's got to be worth a try.

– A window? says Seven.

The kid is eager-eyed. Dumb fucking idiot farmboy.

– If we can get through this gate, he says, shoot the lock or something….

#

Seven hands one shotgun to Matthew, cocks the other and brings it up, but he doesn't aim at the lock. Instead he aims at that square of light, pulls the trigger and blasts it to a shower of glass and sparks.

Broken bulbs and bare wall.

– No, says Matthew, in a small voice.

– We're thirteen levels underground, says Seven. You didn't know?

Matthew shakes his head, raises the shotgun in his hands.

– What the fuck are you—shit!

Seven dives back from the ricochet of shot as Matthew pumps the first barrel into the gate's electronic lock, followed by the second, then swivels the gun to smash the butt into the lock, harder and harder until there's a *clang*. He grabs the door, hauls it open, runs down the corridor, sliding to a stop at the shattered illusion of a window, all wires and filaments and brick wall, nothing more than a screen with a bit of lighting behind it.

– No, he says.

#

A corridor. A window. Bait for anyone stupid enough to walk into a kick in the teeth. Just another way to break a man. Seven turns away in disgust from the boy crumpled to his knees in front of a lie, a lure. He leans a forearm on the storage closet, thuds a fist on it, then steps back, looks at the frame of the door, tries the handle. It's locked, of course. But if they wanted a final twist of the knife, he thinks, to drive it home, how screwed you are and by your own stupidity, your own pathetic....

– Come here, he says.

– Why? says the kid. What's the point?

He stalks down the corridor, hauls the boy up by the collar, drags him to the closet door.

– The day you put on that uniform for real, he says, I'm betting the first thing they do is bring you here and show you this. How close you were.

The first kick splinters the lock. The second smashes the door open, revealing a wide landing, elevators, and a door marked STAIRS.

– You ever seen a closet door that opens inward? says Seven.

#

– Stairs or elevator? says Matthew.

– They'll be waiting for us either way, says Seven. Hostage situation protocol: Evacuate the building; lock down all floors; seal off the perimeter; bring in the SWAT team, snipers on all exits.

Seven stalks the landing, glaring at the elevator doors, the stairwell, the TV in one corner. Matthew can just about see the computations going on.

– Question, says the killer. You're an evil motherfucking demonspawn of Hell and I have one of your minions held at gunpoint. What do you do?

– Like you said. I pull everyone out, put snipers

on every exit, wait for a clear shot to take you down. Right?

– Wrong, says Seven. You pull back, sure, let me take a hostage, try to bargain my way out. But when you get your shot you take the hostage out just to show that you're the baddest bastard around. You don't give a fuck about minions. What *do* you care about?

– Power, says Matthew. Control. How people think.

The TV cuts through shots of a concrete room of scattered bodies, a dead guard in a bath, more corpses in a corridor, Knightly narrating—*gruesome scenes of maniacal malevolence*—from a landing identical to this one.

– We're heading up to the ground floor now to meet the brave men of the HPD, the reporter is saying. In the meantime, here's a word from our sponsors.

Matthew looks at Seven.

– Perception, he says.

#

The Barrage of Battle

– Tired of your pathetic existence? Try Crool-Tea, the refreshing drink of sweet revenge.

Knightly ignores the ad break on the elevator TV, the slow countdown of floors on the display above the door, the nervous glances and guarded stances of the news team and their six-man armed escort, busy arguing on his cellphone.

– Well, we're heading up now…. Look, tell your boss if I'd done that the story would have been shit…. Do I tell you how to run Hell? We're talking modern media here, not frickin' tablets of stone. You need establishing shots, the trail of carnage, human interest. You don't *open* with the frickin' showdown!

#

– You're kidding, says Matthew.

He peers over the edge of the elevator's roof, at the second elevator rising as they descend. The horizontal gap between the two is kind of wide for comfort, and it's a long way down the shaft. A *long* way down. Seven closes the hatch behind him.

– Look on the bright side, he says. There's probably no ground to hit if you miss.

He checks the progress of the other elevator, takes a few steps back.

– You ready?

– No, says Matthew.

– Well, good luck for eternity, chickenshit.

– Aw… jeez, says Matthew.

#

– I like mine served cold! grins a freckle-faced kid in the ad, a bloody baseball bat in one hand, glass of iced tea in the other.

Knightly slaps off the cameraman's tugging hands, bats away the five fingers held up in his face.

– What? Oh.

Four. Three.

– I have to go. I'm on.

Two. He snaps the cellphone shut, as the display over the door changes from *15* to *14*. There's a thump on the ceiling of the elevator, then another. *One.*

– What the fuck was that? says Knightly.

Then the hatch flies open and the gunfire starts.

#

The archangel drums his fingers on his desk. He can't see the carnage in the elevator on his wall of screens, the CCTV in the elevator shot to white noise, and the Vox News camera on its side on the floor, lens spattered in blood, frame filled by the pulped face of one of Knightly's escorts. But he can hear the barrage of battle—shotguns, machine guns, pistols. So can most of Hell.

The archangel rubs his eyes with thumb and forefinger.

– Get up, motherfucker. You got news to report.

The angel looks up. The camera is back in action, a blood-spattered Knightly standing nervously in centre frame, eyes flicking to the left. Someone off-screen gives a low moan that becomes a hacking cough.

– Hello… this is Trent Knightly for Vox News, coming to you from the depths of the Institute, where a rampaging madman—

The sound of a gun being cocked. Knightly glances left again.

– where a crazed killer—

The shotgun barrel comes into frame at the side of his head.

– where an *escaped fugitive* has wreaked bloody slaughter, leaving only myself and one—

The hacking cough becomes a spluttering gargle, cut off with a gunshot, sudden and loud. Knightly flinches.

– leaving only myself alive, he says.

#

A Labyrinth of a Thousand Monsters

Belle holds the door shut, keycard between door and frame to keep the lock from clicking shut. Last thing she wants is to be trapped in this charnel house of a room, same as her own except for the blood soaking the carpet, smeared across the walls in handprints and slogans. The corpse on the sodden bed is a vision of her future, she thinks, if they catch her.

She lets the footsteps pass, then opens the door a crack, peers out as the bellboy turns a corner down the hallway. She slips out after him, following but holding back, staying at each corner till he turns the next, then hurrying after to be sure she doesn't lose him. From the

TV news she knows that the streets are some fucked-up shit, but if the choice is to stay in this hotel of dead-end corridors, numberless rooms of muffled sounds that conjure horrors she tries not to picture, grunting men and screaming women, crying children, squealing animals....

A labyrinth of a thousand monsters, she thinks. She'll take her chances where there's room enough to run.

\#

One wrong turn. Damn. Eli glances left and right along the back-street. There are groups of cops at both ends; the whole area is crawling with them. He can't get caught, *mustn't*. He's heard what they do to membered Forgotten in the Institute, what happens in its lower levels. The shelters are rife with all sorts of rumours of Hell's depths, the *real* demons lurking in layers of rot, millennia of flesh washed by black rain into the sewers, and deeper. Lucifer himself at the very bottom. The Key that'll drive you mad to look at it, knowing you'll never own it.

He ducks down the steps to the basement door. The hobo signs on it are fresh chalk: *not safe at night*; *good pickings*. Doesn't necessarily mean it's safe during daylight, but he needs some sort of cover quick. The padlock on the door is broken, opens in his hand.

He twists it off and slips into the gloom.

\#

Belle sneaks a quick look round the corner; the bellboy steps into the elevator, turns—she ducks back. She waits for the sound of the doors closing, then scopes the corridor again. Clear. She runs to the elevator, punches the button, then flattens herself into the shallow alcove of the doors as, down the hallway, a maid pushes a laundry cart out of a room. The alcove is too shallow to hide her, really, but luckily the maid turns the other way. Wheels squeak as the woman pushes her cart a short distance down the corridor, then turns it towards the wall. She walks round to the front, slides a laundry chute open with a clang, then leans into the cart, and hefts.

Belle turns away, closing her eyes, as the maid struggles the shrouded form out of the cart and into the chute. The *ping* of the elevator returning is a welcome sound.

#

The basement corridor is dank, all unplastered walls with pipes and ducts, a door to the right leading off into a disused laundry room, one wall lined with washers and dryers grimed with dust. Slopes of soiled washing rise against the other wall, items heaped by type—piles of sheets, shirts, underwear—all stinking of semen, piss, shit, worse. Further down to the left, a Lost Property room contains more piles—shoes, spectacles, wallets— some high enough to touch the ceiling. In another, the piles are of bones—femurs, pelvises, skulls. In a fourth, a half dozen dead bodies lie sprawled on a concrete floor that belongs in a slaughterhouse. Eli crouches down before the nearest, closes its vacant eyes, jumps back as another drops out of a chute above his head, hits the floor in a flop of lifeless limbs.

#

Survival of the Baddest

– Listen, whispers Knightly. We can help each other.

The reporter glances furtively at Seven, crouched beside them in the corner of the roof-level landing, attention focused on the camera's viewscreen as he plays back footage of Knightly jumping down from the Vox News copter, the SWAT team deploying in the background. He fast-forwards through shots of armoured men, prefab barricades, rewinds and pauses on a close-up of one cop.

– Well, well, he murmurs.

Knightly's fawning whispers carry on.

– The hostage who saw it all. One call to the right people and I can turn you from a zero to a hero. Chat shows, cocaine and hookers. Give me the exclusive eyewitness report and—

– I'm not a hostage, says Matthew. You're the hostage.

Seven hands the camera to Knightly.

– You're both hostages, he says. Now shut the fuck up. You, get me on the air now.

He drags the body of the last guard from the elevator, strips the tear gas canisters, the grenades, and hooks them to his own vest, slings the man's Uzi over his shoulder.

– What's the plan? says Matthew.

– The plan? says Seven. I'm going to send a message these fuckers will understand. I'm going to kill you both on live TV.

#

– So you *know* there's no hope of escape? whimpers Knightly.

The archangel studies Seven's unblinking visage on the screen.

– That's right, motherfucker, says the hitman. But if the only way out of here is in a body bag, well, I'm taking as many motherfuckers with me as I can, starting with you two. Any last words, whitebread?

The shot pans to the young doctor, down on his knees.

– You don't need to do this. Please, this is crazy.

– Fuck *need*. I told you before, kid, I am a *very* bad man.

The camera swings back to Seven.

– You dig what I'm saying, motherfuckers? No negotiations. No hostages. Just you and me.

The shotguns rise, one pointed straight to camera, the other to the side.

– Bring it.

With a flash and a boom, the screen turns to noise. The archangel swears under his breath, then picks up his cellphone, dials.

– Take him down. Now.

#

– Shit! says Knightly. Frickin' Jesus—

Matthew opens his eyes just in time to see Seven floor the idiot with the butt of his shotgun. He fumbles the gas mask Seven tosses at him as he clambers to his feet, confused.

– Put it on. Don't make me regret this, whitebread.

– What are you doing?

– You think these motherfuckers earned Hell with a glorious death in the line of duty? Shit, these are the kind of pantywaist assholes who'll beat up a brother for a broken tail light, shoot some poor bastard for looting diapers during a disaster, kill a kid who points his water pistol at them. The kind who lose it when the gunfire starts, dig? I've met bad cops, kid. A bad cop is a chickenshit with a badge and gun. Now get back and stay down.

Matthew pulls the gas mask on, as Seven fits his own. He backs away, watches Seven pick Knightly up by his belt and collar, heave him out through the swing doors.

– Aw, jeez, says Matthew.

Seven rolls to one side as bullets batter the doors, shatter the windows. Canisters spin in through the empty frames, bounce off the walls, and roll across the floor, spewing gas.

– Aw jeez, says Matthew again, diving to the floor as the gunfire starts for real.

\#

Seven scatters the tear gas canisters like he's Santa Claus throwing gifts to the kiddies. Motherfuckers will be masked up, but at least the gas will cover him. He dives out the door and rolls, comes out on his feet and running, spraying the Uzi, throwing more tear gas, this way and that, presents for everyone, baby, grenades for the best-behaved. Jumping a sandbag barricade into the chaos of smoke lit by the flash of gunfire, shadows in the mist, he's got one advantage. For them, every hint of a human form might be a colleague not to kill in the crossfire. For him? Everything's a target.

It's not a great advantage given that there's one of him and a fuckload of them, but hey, it's Hell, and these pig motherfuckers wouldn't be here if they had a fucking spine. Besides, odds don't mean shit in a logic of impossibilities, mazes of corridors that don't make any sense, fuck knows what else. And if this is the logic of nightmares, Seven reckons, in that logic the monsters always win.

This is survival of the baddest.

So he just has to be the baddest motherfucker of them all.

\#

The Streets of Hell

Belle slips her heels off, scopes the lobby. If the cops in the bar aren't enough, there's the doorman, the concierge, the reception desk, way too many people between her and the front door. She's safe for now, the elevator recess in the back corner of the lobby out of their line of sight, but the floor display behind her is counting down, so she has to move fast or she's screwed anyway. The only other option is the doorway in the opposite recess. A few seconds' exposure. Armchairs in the lobby that might work as cover. The receptionists are chatting. The concierge turns—fuck it, now! She goes for it, running fast and low, bare feet quiet on the carpet. She hits the alcove, pushes through the door, into a stairwell.

The stairs lead down past a "staff only" sign. She doesn't stop to check if she's been followed till she's at the bottom, where a fire door with a rattling bar of a handle opens into a corridor lit by bare bulbs, grimed with filth. The stairwell above is quiet. She slides her heels on. There's got to be another way out, a service entrance.

She passes doors, some locked, others opening into stenches too vile to stomach. Like the floors above, the layout… doesn't quite add up, but she keeps moving, through a boiler room, down another corridor. Over a generator's hum and rattling pipes, she hears distant footsteps, the creak of a door, other sounds—human or animal—noises she hopes are being carried down through ventilation ducts from above.

She tests a door to her right and it opens a crack, to a glimpse of—

– You don't want to go in there.

Belle stumbles as she spins, feels a hand on her arm—belongs to a big guy, dressed like he's wearing everything he owns. Smells like he doesn't take it off to shit. She shakes off his grip.

– Fuck, she says. Fucking….

As he shuts the door, the vision slowly registers on her mind's eye: bones and blood. She crosses herself, and the tramp cocks his head.

– Faith in Hell? he mumbles. You sure you belong here, girl?

– I'm visiting from out of town, she says.

#

– Come on, says Seven.

Matthew pokes his head through the doors. Out on the roof, Seven is crouching down to flip Knightly over. A hard slap gets a moan from the reporter, a flicker of eyelids. Another brings him fully round, blinking, then shoving himself back, sliding on gore. There's a lot of gore to slide on.

– Don't kill me, says Knightly. I can give you coverage.

– Shut the fuck up and get on that phone. You call your copter down here now, and you get us the fuck out of this city.

Seven stands, aims his Uzi at Knightly's balls.

– And don't tell me it's not possible.

As Knightly taps out a number, punches the dial button, Matthew gazes over the carnage, the roof a battlefield of bodies, smoke and rubble, flames rising from copters with police decals still visible in the wreckage. Seven kicks a severed arm off the scorched, stained landing pad, barely discernable as a red cross in the centre of a wide white circle. Overhead, the Vox News copter circles.

– If he *doesn't* land, Knightly is saying, *I'll* feed him to a frickin' cab.

After a moment's pause, the Vox News copter starts to descend. Seven grabs the phone from Knightly, snaps it shut, and throws it off the roof.

#

– It's not safe here, says Eli.

– No shit, says Belle.

She ties the bootlace and stands, walks over to another hoard of goods stripped from, she's all too sure, the corpses of the hotel's… clients? guests? victims?

fuck knows, she thinks. Whoever owned them doesn't need them now; that's all that matters. She scavenges an overcoat, worn but decent, flicks it on. Least it'll cover the crack-whore chic of the rest of her wardrobe.

– It's not safe outside either, says Eli. The cops....

– I know *all* about the cops, she says. But *you* survive out there, right?

– It's easier if you're forgotten, he says.

– Um, yeah, she says. OK.

She looks at him, the skid row chic, the thousand-yard stare. He's clearly cracked, but broken-crazy, she figures, not bad-crazy. She pulls the belt of her overcoat tight. With his rummaged clothes, the down-and-out smells a *little* less like something that crawled out of the sewers. But three coats is still two too many.

– The idea is *not* to stand out, she says. To blend in.

His gaze is blank like she's talking a foreign language. Talking fucking *sense*, she thinks. How this crazy bastard has survived at all, she can't imagine.

– Fuck it, she says. Let's just get out of here.

\#

– You don't get it, the pilot shouts. *No Fly Zone*, shithead. *No. Fly. Zone.*

Seven steadies himself as the copter banks right, heading uptown through grey canyons of skyscraper shells. Down in the streets of Hell, crowds crawl over pile-ups, stream along the sidewalks, and he wonders what kind of torture Hell has for the little sinners. Hovel homes? Wage slave workplaces? Up in front, beside the pilot, Matthew keeps lookout for police. Beside Seven, Knightly is quiet, bound and gagged with gaffer tape to give everyone fucking peace. The pilot's taken over asshole duty though, laughs, casual in his disregard of the shotgun barrel aimed at his head.

– We're talking state-of-the-art surface-to-air guided

missiles, he says. We take this bird past the city limits, they blow us outta the fuckin' sky. You're screwed, shithead; you're just too fuckin' dumb to see it.

He swings the copter left, round another corner.

– So what now, dumbass? Keep flying round and round till we're outta gas? They're *gonna* find you. They're gonna drag you back to your own personal shithole, then—

Seven presses the shotgun-barrel to the side of his face.

– You are seriously pissing me off, motherfucker.

The pilot shrugs it off with a roll of shoulders.

– Fuck you. Shoot me, this bird drops like a fuckin' stone. Some escape plan. Body bags to freedom! Oh, yeah.

Seven snarls.

– You just set us down somewhere quiet, dig? he says. Somewhere the cops don't go.

– You're not in Harlem now, Shaft. Where the cops don't go, fuck, you don't wanna know. You got no idea what this place is, shithead, no fuckin' idea.

They swing right again and Matthew leans forward. The pilot twists over the back of his seat to grin at Seven.

– You wanna see this city's heart? he says. I'll show you somewhere *nobody* goes.

Matthew's words are almost a whisper.

– Oh my….

– Motherfucker, says Seven as the scale of what's ahead sinks in.

#

An Urge to Jump

Belle clambers up over the car's hood onto the roof, boots clomping on the metal. Six cars high, fuck knows how deep, the wall of piled-up wrecks still blocks her vision. Running off to the left maybe four blocks or more, she figures, it turns a sharp ninety degrees ahead of her, disappearing off into the distance. Judging by the skyline that runs parallel to it both ways, they're at the corner of some levelled area in the city's heart. Fuck, it must be fucking huge. Behind her, the intersection and the roads that edge the great wall form a junkyard warren of lower heaps. In this little clearing on the edge of it, Eli squats at the base of a pedestal that's long since lost its statue, studying graffiti like a hunter reading tracks. She climbs down.

– You sure that shit means something? she says.

– Hobo signs, he says. You don't forget just because you're forgotten.

She scratches at one arm. It could be fleas in the scavenged clothes making her skin crawl, but the growing nausea and the sweat.... Fuck.

– Whatever, she says. What does it say?

– There's a safe place close, he says. Where nobody goes.

#

She follows him round a heap of rusted hulks, clambers over another and squeezes through a gap after him, down a narrow passage. Every so often he stops to check another sign in paint or scratchwork, or to check that she's still with him.

– You OK? he says.

– I'm fine, she lies. You sure this is safe?

– Nobody comes here, he says.

– Why not?

He scrambles up a slope of cars, angles through a tight gap in the great wall of wrecks, and she follows, through the break in the wall and... vertigo hits her in the gut, an urge to jump, to clutch at the nearest scrap of solidity, to fall. The wall slopes down on the other side, fifty feet or so, to where….

The ground drops away into a gaping, ragged-edged mouth of dark. Four blocks wide or more, yeah, too long even to guess, and too deep to imagine, the chasm before her looks like someone took a knife to the city, cut its heart loose in four strokes and punched it out to drop away into the darkness forever. The darkness *of* forever. Central Pit, she thinks.

– You stare into it long enough, says Eli, feels like it's staring back.

He starts to climb down. She registers the sound of the copter, takes it as a spur to keep moving, following him down. Far below, the twisted rails of a subway line jut out into the emptiness.

– Where the fuck are you going?

– Signs say it's this way. Shelter.

– I thought you said nobody comes here?

– Lots of nobodies in Hell, says Eli.

#

They're still a good ten feet above the clearing when Knightly makes his break for it, jumping from the copter, hitting the ground in a roll.

– Shit!

Seven grabs the Uzi with his left hand, fires a burst at the motherfucker, pounds the tarmac at his feet but misses the reporter. Fuck. He swings out of his seat, jumps down into the junkyard, fires a blast from the shotgun in his right hand just as Knightly dives over the hood of a car. Fuck! As he reaches the car, Knightly is already leaping over the boot of another, sprinting for the corner of a building.

– Seven!

The kid's behind him, pointing up at the copter now rising, angling away, the pilot making for the sky. No way, motherfucker. He strides back towards the clearing, guns blasting at the copter, bullets and shot punching the fuselage, shattering glass as the machine swings round. For a second it keeps rising; then it veers, off-kilter. Seven is vaguely aware of the kid running towards him, then skidding to a halt, diving to one side as Seven's firing line follows the copter down.

The explosion is satisfying, but as he turns away the downside comes clear; the fucking reporter's long gone.

The kid clears his throat.

– You know, the whole burning helicopter wreck, he says, it does kinda say, *this way to the fugitives*.

– Take a look around you, whitebread, says Seven. It'll fit right in.

#

Seven squeezes down the lane of scorched and rusted husks after Matthew, dubious of the kid's memory of a route glimpsed from the copter, but in no doubt at all that it's just a matter of time before Knightly gets word to the Powers Below of where they are, where they're headed.

– So why *didn't* you kill us both? says Matthew. Back in the Institute?

Seven shrugs, but the question kind of irks him 'cause he doesn't have an answer. No point throwing away potential assets, he thinks. Somewhere inside, he knows that's bullshit. So why? Because whatever these motherfuckers want from him, he's not going to play their game?

– You remind me of a kid I knew, he says eventually.

Matthew pulls himself up a wall of cars.

– Someone you killed?

– Someone I *didn't* kill, he says. A witness. Didn't know enough to keep his mouth shut, earned himself a hit. I let him run.

– Maybe you're not so bad.

Foot in a window frame, Seven pushes past the kid, snorting. Yeah, sure. We're buddies now, together in adversity. He reaches for a grip.

– I cut his thumbs off, he says. Told him to disappear or it'd be his balls next, and that if he even thought of testifying they'd be his last meal before the bullet. So, hey, maybe I *am* capable of mercy.

He doesn't look back for the reaction, but he can't help a sly smile as he pulls himself up to the roof of the top car in the wall. Cornball kid.

– Shit, he says.

Looking out across the abyss at all the layers of streets, sewers, and subways, the strata of city exposed like roots, worm trails and buried litter in the wall of a grave cut by a giant's shovel, Seven, for the first time, feels just a little outmatched. This is Hell they're up against.

– They went down, says Matthew. Over here.

#

Being and Not Being

The flicker of firelight up ahead in the tunnel gives Eli's shadow solidity, something more to stumble after than the sound of feet scuffling over rubble, but Belle is too strung out to really care now. Even as the distant circle of warm gold in the dark grows closer, and the glint of rails and sleepers tells her where to put her feet so she doesn't fall again, it's the shakes and the hunger that fill her mind. The need. She pushes herself on.

The tunnel opens up to an old station lit by candles here and there, beds of rags tucked tight to the walls at the side of stairwells, under or on top of benches. Looks like some refugee camp. Only the refugees heard them coming and thought better of playing host to visitors.

She figures that's probably a good survival strategy in Hell.

– Forgotten shelter, says Eli, climbing up onto the platform.

– What? she says.

He reaches a hand down to Belle, hauls her up.

– You can't see them, but—[he turns, talks to thin air]—what? No.

She leans on an old subway map display, where washed-out lines trace the island's grid of streets, the black rectangle of the pit at its heart. There are scribbles inked all over it, she notices, an X on a bridge crossing from the east side to a grey shore labelled LIMBO, a hash sign in the dotted line of a tunnel leading west to a faded NEW JER....

– They're not happy about us being here, Eli says, but they won't—[he turns again]—you know we won't harm you. Just for one night.

Belle looks around at the empty platform.

– *Right*, she says slowly.

She feels another wave of nausea hit, retches.

– You're sick, he says.

– Yeah, she says. Fuck, yeah.

#

Matthew jumps for the umpteenth time since they entered the tunnels, spooked by another glimpse out of the corner of his eye. Half-seen snatches of shapes in motion. Shades in the dark. The light of Seven's makeshift torch dances on stone slick and lurid with mineral dissolution, rust-red and pale-green streaks and stains, the slow rivulet of a drop. It can't be just the light playing tricks on him.

– I'm not imagining this, he says.

– Sure, kid, says Seven. Ghosts in Hell.

A moan echoes down the tunnel, and Seven lowers

his torch. Beyond him, up in front, there's a glimmer in the dark, softer than daylight. Matthew holds his tongue; Seven's not the kind of man who takes kindly to *I told you so*. He follows the killer towards the glow, the firelight resolving into the edge of an old subway platform, tiles and steel, dust and graffiti, blankets. Matthew spots the woman—the one he saw from the copter—huddled against a pillar now, eyes closed, body shaking. He jumps up onto the platform.

– Miss, he says, you OK?

The man steps out of the shadow of a stairwell.

#

– Don't move, motherfucker, says Seven. Nice and chill.

He keeps the shotgun trained on the hobo as he slides himself up onto the platform, rises.

– You don't need the gun here, brother, says the man. We're no threat.

– I'm not your brother, says Seven. And I'll decide who's a threat.

Wild beard and hair of a desert baptist or a down-and-out, the man meets his gaze with the unblinking stare of someone who lost himself long ago. After a cold moment of evaluation, Seven lowers the gun.

The kid hunkers down beside the woman. She's not bad-looking in a pale and wasted jailbait sorta way, but…. Seven knows the signs.

– Cold turkey, he says. Right?

She nods, leans to one side to retch. The kid shuffles back.

– Jeez.

– *Jeez?* she coughs. Are you for real?

She sizes the two of them up, eyes narrowing.

– You're the runner, right? she says to Seven. Broke out of some hospital? Don't suppose you picked up any painkillers?

– No, he says.

– Figures. Shit, this isn't going to be good.

#

– Please, sobs Belle. Just let me go. I can find what I need. Please, I just….

Eli cradles her as the struggling breaks to sobs, more accusations, and pleas. He does his best, but between the shits and shakes there's only one thing on her mind: getting the junk back into her blood. He pushes hair back from her face.

– It's OK, he says.

Seven and Matthew are over at the subway map, studying it, talking in low voices. Seven glances back at Eli and Belle.

– …extra baggage, he's saying.

– You're not the only one wants out of here, says the boy.

– I'm the only one I give a fuck about.

– It's OK, says Eli. It'll be OK.

He's not talking to Belle, though. It's the other accusations and pleas he's dealing with: You brought them here; they don't belong here; you have to go, please; this is our place, ours; you'll lead them here; you have no right.

The mob of Forgotten crowd him with incessant voices. Membered but still… *marginal*, Eli still sees the others, if only just, like ghosts. To hear them clearly he has to… lose a little of himself. Sometimes now their words slip past and all he recalls afterwards is an angry tone, a grabbing hand. Sometimes he thinks he's imagining it all, mad as the others think he is. A crazy man talking to thin air.

– Please, just a few hours more, he says. A day.

– Get out!

Eli closes his eyes, torn between two surrenders: to be fully like the others, driving the Forgotten from his mind; or to forget *himself* again and hope that Hell will follow suit. So he cradles Belle as she moans in her own fevered struggle between being and not being.

ACT THREE-ATTACK

A Crucible of Souls

This is Hell: fire in the veins of a junky whore; skin burning, crawling with insect itch; toxic sweat seeping, soaking the world with a stink of pus and piss; spasms of vomit; arched back and white knuckles; broken fingernails scratching at the arms that hold you; a suffering without dignity; the destruction of identity; a breaking down of body and soul to primal elements of need; the need for food; the need for sleep; the denial of both; the furious delirium of the beast; the scream of an animal giving birth to itself.

The fire that burns away even need, until all that's left is a quiet nothing that opens its eyes, trembling and weak, but newborn.

\#

This is Hell: voices in the head of a wino; trying to hold on to a scrap of self; trying to forget it, dissolve it, destroy it; clutching a girl who thinks she's a woman because her pain is solid; needing to be needed; soothing and never being soothed; being a rock for others to cling to; saying nothing as they shiver and ask who you are; saying nothing of the false hope of a white light, and a waiting family; being nothing.

Being only one voice of many in your head, letting them drown you in *their* desperation, until the shell of you is almost free of its history, *almost*.

\#

This is Hell: the stalking of a killer caged; cold equations of necessity that don't work out; plans that can't succeed; impossibilities of escape thrown back in your face by a motherfucking cornball kid; being holed up like a fucking rat with a junky, a wino, and this fucking *kid*;

the worthless, useless baggage of others; having this fucking junky ask if there's a way out and not having an answer; seeing the new determination in her eyes; seeing your own reflection in a wino's blank stare as he mutters to his inner demons.

Losing control so that this dumb kid's question has you gripping him by the throat, telling *him* to find a motherfucking way out.

#

This is Hell: the weakness of a boy afraid of the only hope of escape; looking at a murderer, a monster, and seeing something he needs but can't accept; being drawn to strength, to sin; lying to yourself about the why of it; creating disdain by needing; hating what you need; needling a killer to make him notice you, pushing buttons to create hate in return, as a bond.

Until you're standing with a pistol in your hand to prove yourself, blowing a tin can from the edge of the platform and turning back to look at him, puffed-up with fake pride at your *usefulness*.

– I come from Wyoming. You think I don't know how to shoot?

And there's just a little bit of grudging respect in his disdain.

This is Hell, its fires a crucible of souls.

#

Sacrifice or Surrender

The Lord of Hell cradles his ball of light in one hand, phone in the other. On the TV screen, Knightly revels in the unrest caused by the escape. Riots are breaking out all over the city, cops clashing with citizens, citizens attacking cops. Some of the monkeys are inspired by the breakout, taking hope from it; others are enraged by the incompetence of the authorities, furious at others doing what they can't. The story might well play out beautifully in the end—the more hope you raise, after all, the deeper the despair when it's lost—but the archangel prefers his chaos a little more organised. On the screen, cops drag a group of rioters towards waiting vans. One rioter breaks free, makes a run for the camera.

– They say there's no way out, he shouts. No escape! But they're lying! They just want you to believe that, *need* you to—

The man's blood sprays the camera lens.

It's the third day of the fugitives being on the run, and the archangel is listening patiently as the Chief of Police explains how close they are now. Took them a while to track down Knightly in the entertainment district, break him free of his… fans. But now they know where the fugitives were headed, it's only a matter of time.

– Don't take forever, says the angel.

#

– Listen, says Eli. Hear that?

– More radio signals on your fillings? says Seven.

– He's right, says Belle.

Voices echo down the tunnel, vague and distant. Belle can only just discern it, but *only just* is enough.

– Cops, she says.

– Shit, says Seven. We've got to go, now.

– Eli, says Belle. How do we get out of here? You know this place. Is there another way out?

The tramp is muttering apologies at the air, shaking his head. Belle grabs him, tries to make him focus, but he just looks at her in confusion, then shrugs her off and stalks off into the shadows, mumbling—*you can help us… no… and is this any better?… you call this life?*

– Fuck this, says Seven. There's got to be an exit to the surface.

He heads for the nearest stairwell. Matthew hesitates, then follows, but Belle… shit, she can't just leave the tramp, even if he is crazy.

– Wait, she says. Look, wait.

– No! calls Eli.

Seven stops, and Eli's word hangs in the air, a moment of stillness between them. A statement of certainty in his silence.

– That exit's sealed, says Eli. This way.

#

Beams of flashlights scythe the darkness. Boots crunch on gravel and garbage. Gordon cricks his neck and rolls his shoulder, settling the flak jacket. Up front, the lieutenant waves a couple of the others forward, but Gordon hangs back, glancing over his shoulder at the blackness behind them.

Calls of excitement up ahead, discovery. The lieutenant:

– Come on! Move in!

He follows the rest of them into the subway station, noting the candles and the rags everywhere. There's no sign of the fugitives as he jumps up onto the platform but something isn't—he stumbles, grabs a pillar to steady himself—his back's against it now—shadows on the stairwell—the lieutenant tripping—others turning— what the fuck?

– Shit!

He rips the camcorder from his belt, swings it up, switching it on. All around them ragged shades are scattering, the whole place a fucking rat's nest of Forgotten, and every jostle a jump cut in memory, a moment lost. He's opening fire—not the only one but—he's turned around—nearly shoots the fucking lieutenant—shit!

Concentration fractured by the breaks, it takes him a second to realise it's not just the rats fleeing their nest, the shoves and shoulderings, bump and jostle of panic.

It's a fucking attack. No way. This can't be happening.

His finger squeezes the trigger of his submachine gun, stays squeezed as he fires wildly at these fucking scraps of human beings who've never had the guts to stand up for themselves in the whole history of Hell.

#

Gunfire behind them, they jog on, Eli in front, torch in his hand, bitter despair in his thoughts, the voice of one of the Forgotten cutting over the others: *You brought them down on us, you fucker.* And then a shift in that voice, something lost, something found, a new hope or the end of it all: *Make it fucking worth it.* Now he leads the others through the darkness, away from the noise of suicides that might be sacrifice or surrender.

– I hope you know where we're going, *brother*.

He ignores Seven's scorn. Belle whisper a response he misses.

– Yeah, directions from imaginary friends, says Seven. Real inspiring.

Another whisper.

– All I want is to know where the fuck we're going. What do you say, *brother?* Want to clue us in?

– There are other havens, says Eli. Places to hide. We just need to keep moving.

– Hide and seek? Fuck that. What we want is a fucking way out.

– There's no way out, says Eli. Those are just stories.

Stories told by the Forgotten, Eli thinks, huddling in their shelters, lying to each other as much to share their misery as anything. *Hey, buddy. You're new, right? You heard about the Key? No? Well, hey, give us a smoke and I'll tell you about it. Yeah. See, here's the story....* And then some tall tale about some brave Forgotten, a journey to the deepest levels of the city. A story of grit and gumption, a hobo hero trying to cut a deal with the devil. A story that's all just a set-up for the bitter twist, the grisly fate. *And the stupid fucker's still there screaming. 'Cause there is no fucking way out, dipshit. Whaddaya think, buddy? Ain't that a fucking peachy story?*

– What stories, motherfucker? says Seven.

And though he knows it's bitterness he's acting on, Eli tells him.

Seven's reaction is not what he expects.

#

Into the Lion's Den

– You two are nuts, says Belle. Did you even listen to him? The stories are just another way to twist the knife. Shit, even if they're true, the message is *don't fuck with the system.*

Seven climbs the steps behind her and Eli.

– *Leatherwing Satanspawn*, he says, *nightmares made flesh.* Only horns here are on the motherfucking taxis, honey. I ain't buying this bogeyman bullshit.

– But the magic Key to open the Gates of Hell, she says, *that* you believe?

Matthew is beside him as they come out into the dark concourse. Broken signs lettered in fading primary colours catch the firelight. Tunnels of tiling behind them and off to the side. Turnstiles ahead.

– Maybe the lies are *close* to the truth, says the kid. Maybe they're giving you a chance to pass up, just so one day they can shove your face in it.

Last person Seven expected to be on his wavelength is the kid, but they both remember a way out marked "storage," an exit in plain view. *That's* how they twist the knife here. He moves up past Belle, slaps a hand against a barred gate.

– It's the doors that make a prison, he says, not the walls. The doors you don't even *try* to open.

#

He pushes through a turnstile, waits for Eli.

– You got us where I said, right?

Eli nods, and Seven walks on, the exit ahead a little lighter in the darkness. Steps lead up to a padlocked gate, a sign for 666th Avenue South. There's noise beyond— sirens, shots, and screams of the infernal city.

– Shit, how you gonna even get down to these *lower levels?* says Belle. Parachute down the Pit?

Seven takes a shot at the padlock, then swings the shotgun's butt down on the broken remnants, hauls the gate open, takes the steps two at a time, staying close to the wall and keeping an eye out for passers-by. All the bustle is across the intersection though, around the monolith of a building that must take up a whole city block at least.

– Fuck the Pit, says Seven. I'm taking the elevator.

#

Matthew pulls up his collar against rain that's cold and black as the night itself, too thin for oil but like no water he's ever seen. It runs off their clothes, but it pools in the gutters like ink, reflecting the streetlights and the cars, the flashing blues and reds of ambulances, cop cars, fire trucks… and the great stone overhang engraved with lettering that spells out simply THE INSTITUTE, mirrored at his feet. He raises his eyes, looks across at all the grey uniforms of Hell's once-human demons, running between the vehicles, pushing stretchers with patients in straitjackets and hoods. New arrivals.

– Motherfuckers, says Seven.

On either side of the parking bay, cop cars and fire trucks are coming up out of ramps every minute or so, heading out into the night. As they watch, an ambulance returns, siren wailing; its doors swing open, spill out a team of paramedics and a stretcher with a shuddering body bag on it. As they batter it through swing doors into the ER, Matthew feels a chill of sick panic twist his stomach, shiver his spine.

#

– You still want to follow me through the fire, whitebread? says Seven.

– I still want out of here, says Matthew.

– So what's your grand plan, boys? says Belle. Walk into the lion's den with a bullwhip and a chair? I'll take my chances on the street if—

– I'm going in with you, says Eli.

– What the fuck?

Belle's words are matched by Seven's stare, and Matthew's as surprised as either of them. Eli stands staring at the doors of the ER, where another DOA is being wheeled in, doctors bitching about *more paperwork*. There's no expression on his face... none that Matthew can read.

– Shit, says Belle.

Whatever she's thinking, she's no more readable than Eli.

– You think they got drugs in there? she says eventually.

#

A Stupid Plan

In the radius of fear around the Institute the buildings are mostly vacant, but for the odd shop or strip joint among the shells. Belle drums her fingers on the phone booth's side. The only others on the streets are three-in-the-morning drunks—off-duty doctors and death squads, brawling long since turned to bawling—but still.... One cop crawls along the sidewalk now, tears and blood and black rain streaming down his face. He grabs at Seven's legs, pleads for the mercy he's forgotten how to give. It just breaks Belle's heart. It just breaks her fucking heart that the bastard is so wasted, so self-degraded, she could cut his throat and he'd probably just mouth *thank you* as he died. Seven kicks the man towards the gutter, and she turns back to Matthew.

If this is going to work, she's going to need to be convincing.

– So what were you in there for? she says. You said they were trying to cure you, right? What of?

#

– Nothing, says Matthew. They were wrong.

He avoids the arched-eyebrow look she shoots him, but finds Seven's stare just as bad. He follows Eli's gaze, down the street the way they came.

– It's *Hell*, he says. They just mess with your head here, try to—

– Bullshit! says Seven. I kill people and they give me prison, the lady of the night gets a cheap hotel, and Captain Hobo gets the streets. You get hospital. Why?

– It doesn't mean anything.

Belle points the receiver at him.

– Tell it to the swim squad, farmboy. You wouldn't be here if you weren't a fuck-up like the rest of us. What was it? Steroids? Date rape? Fucked your sister? The family dog? Give.

Matthew gazes through the shutters over the gun shop window, doesn't even meet his own reflection's eye. It's none of their business.

– Use your imagination, he says.

#

Belle mutters a curse as she turns back to the phone, taps for a dial tone, punches 911. Shit, worst that can happen is they all end up in eternal torment, right? She nearly laughs, stops herself as the electronic voice starts on the other end of the line. Then music. Then finally—

– Yeah, hello, I need an ambulance.

Matthew stays stony-faced as she gives the operator the address, then starts spinning her line—some kid out in the street, acting crazy, ranting, smashing shit up, you know, like he needs treatment. No, it seems like more than just anger. *What is he ranting about?* She glowers at the boy but he's saying nothing. Fucking… shit.. Got to give them something….

She grins. Starts telling the operator just how crazy this kid *gotta* be, you know, to say what he's saying, in *this* place. Then:

– I mean… he keeps saying that there's no God.

Matthew and Seven are both watching her as she hangs up.

– Atheism, right? These fuckers gotta see that as a mental illness.

#

The ambulance's siren winds down but the lights are still flashing as the vehicle's two-man paramedic team and doctor jump down, Belle at their side immediately, pointing them at Matthew. Not that the boy is inconspicuous, standing out in the centre of the intersection, screaming about aliens and mass hallucination. As the medics move in to restrain him, Eli answers Seven's flick of head with a nod and the two of them slide out of the shadow of the gun shop doorway. Belle is already moving back from the melee, catching the driver's eye while Seven and Eli edge up the sides of the vehicle towards the doors. When Eli's hand slaps the passenger window the man starts.

Eli motions for him to wind the window down; when the driver just shakes his head, waves him away, he starts pounding glass with the heels of his fists, harder and faster. All Eli has to do is drum loud enough to hide the click of the driver's door as the man reaches under his seat, brings out a stun-baton. Seven, reaching in through the open door, does the rest, quick as a click of fingers.

The image of the driver's lolling head stays with Eli as Belle pulls him to the back of the ambulance and in, places a gun in his hand.

– Come on, she's saying. Earth to Eli.

Then Seven is there as well, and the three of them are sat in the back, weapons trained on the paramedics at the doors now, shock on their faces.

Through the stripping and binding, gagging and clubbing of the captives, it's the vacant stare of the dead driver Eli thinks of, how for all the horror he's seen here this is the first he's been a part of.

– We ready to go? asks Belle.

Buttoning his paramedic uniform, Eli looks to the others for their confirmations. Matthew nods. Seven crouches at the shuttered doorway of the gun store, a little piece of wire in his hand.

– If we're going to fuck with Hell, he says, we want a little extra firepower.

\#

A Place of Panic

Just another ambulance pulling up into a bay that's full of them. Just another paramedic team dragging a gurney out into the chaos. Just another new arrival in a body bag, thrashing against its confines, its muffled rage adding to the tumult. Play it hard and fast. Don't give them time to question. That's what she tells herself as they punch through the double doors and into the ER, her in front, clipboard in hand, cursing their way—Come on! Move it! Coming through! We got a code black here!—speed and noise, *confusion* all she's got to clear a path for them through—sweet Jesus!

\#

There are orderlies siphoning off the new arrivals,

wheeling them away to the personal hells of elsewhere in the Institute, but the ER is a hell in its own right: a reception area of doctors and nurses fighting over gurneys like gulls over carrion; interns carrying corpses back and forth, stumbling under the weight and the weariness; corridors of the dying—scab-crusted patients abandoned to their straps and tubes all along the walls; locked waiting rooms where men, women, and children pound the windows, sobbing for release; operating rooms as torture chambers with bloody floors and bloody walls, filled with sounds of drills and bone-saws; recovery rooms where amputees strain to drag themselves through filth, on stumps, towards the door. It's Hell as a place of panic, she realises.

\#

Matthew keeps his head down, hands white-knuckled on the gurney's side, praying that Belle can pull this off with her curses, claims, and commands. She throws out demands for directions too imperious to be denied, a dozen contradictory excuses for why they can't hand over the patient—this one's going straight up to surgery—straight *down* to surgery?—that's what I said—get that shit out of the way! As far as the orderlies and interns are concerned, it seems, she's got to be a demon, right? And she doesn't give them time to think twice.

So this junky hooker carves them a path through fear and confusion, to the doors of the elevator that will take them down into the depths of Hell.

\#

The doors slide open and a workman comes out, one hand filled with broken electronics, the other holding a phone up to his ear.

– Orders from below? Yeah, well, orders don't mean shit without the fucking *parts*.

Matthew notices a red-haired orderly in the elevator

glancing up as they enter, catches a glimpse of the side of his face before Eli blocks his line of sight; it's only then that the image registers and his heart skips a beat. He leans round a little to sneak a peek as the doors close, jerks back when the orderly turns to Belle.

– Going down?

The voice clinches it, but too late; Red is clearly processing his own recognition, brows unfurrowing to shock as he does a double take, angles past Eli, and grabs Matthew by the shoulder to swing him round. The punch that comes with the swing, square in the orderly's face, is as much a surprise to Matthew as it is to Red.

– Guess so, says Belle as the orderly staggers back and crumples to the floor.

#

Going Down

The elevator descends. Seven clicks a clip into the automatic and hands it to the kid. He reaches into the body bag, pulls out a clip for the Uzi, slaps it in and hands the gun to Belle. Lying on a small arsenal wasn't exactly Shiatsu for his back but they're going to need every motherfucking bullet and cartridge, he reckons. So... a shotgun, an Uzi, and a pistol each. Might be overkill in the land of the living, but fuck knows down here.

Eli shakes his head.

– I don't know, he says. I'm not really....

– Just think of it as carrying my spares, says Seven.

Belle's hand plays with the rosary.

– No pardons or parole in Hell, he says. Prayer won't put *Him* on our side.

Belle looks at the cross like she didn't even know she was holding it.

– Maybe He wants someone to kick Lucifer's ass, she says.

– What do you think it'll be like? says the kid.

Seven shrugs.

– Alcatraz? he says. Auschwitz? What's the worst place you can imagine?

The elevator shudders to a halt. The doors ping and slide open.

– Not this, says the kid.

#

The dereliction of a level left unused for decades. Broken tiles and scattered papers, puddles thick with dust and pulp, the place looks like the last it saw of human life was in a riot a hundred years ago. Matthew helps Eli wheel the gurney between the elevator doors—from the body bag, Red gives a semiconscious moan—then follows Seven and Belle out onto the landing.

The floor is hard and plain as concrete but darker, flecked with white, like clay with ash and bone mixed in. Walls tiled in the same ceramic but glazed and damp, slick as with sweat or saliva. Gas pipes and lighting, flames tinged blue, a smell of methane in the air. A smell of mould and earth. The sound of their own footsteps, soft scuffles and splashes as they spread out and move forward warily.

The layout's not unlike the ER—offices off the corridors, cells with steel doors, operating rooms where the grey is accented with red-brown, rust of tables and trays of surgical tools, and a reception area at the heart of it, the burnt remnants of a desk and more soiled paperwork strewn to decay. Where the doors would be up on the surface level, splintered wood frames only flat grey wall. Like it opened to the outside world once, maybe. Like this lower level wasn't dug out of the ground but swallowed by it, the Institute sinking, buried under its own weight.

#

– So far, so bullshit, says Seven. No army of darkness. No brood of bogeymen. Speak up if you see a dead janitor, 'cause that'll be the archfiend Satan. Motherfucker's probably got the Key on a fucking ring with—

Belle shushes him, hand up—*wait*. After finding squat in the wings off the reception area, the corridors to the back seemed simply more of the same at first, but the deeper in they go the eerier it gets—empty cells with ripped padding on the walls, feathers in the filth, straitjackets and chains, and red-brown smears that might be more than rust. No one else has mentioned it, but she'd swear there's a slope to the corridors; they're going down. And—

– You hear that? she says. What the fuck is that sound?

A siren waver so faint only the peaks of pitch and volume are audible over the drip of pipes. Then, too clear and close to mistake, an answer or echo, ragged as a cat's yowl or a baby's wail.

– Fuck me, says Seven. I'd say that's exactly the sort of creepy shit you don't want to hear in an abandoned lunatic asylum.

– I'm not sure it's abandoned, says Matthew. It's just that all the doors are open.

– That's really not comforting.

#

WHAT DREAMS MAY COME. As they approach the T-junction, Eli hears the words daubed on the wall as a whisper, turns; but there's no Forgotten down here, and the echoes they all can't help but notice now are senseless, moans and sobs. He realises it's his own lips, his own breath, moving in memory of… *Shakespeare in the Park, a summer day, himself a student prince, Sarah coming up afterwards to—*

The boy walks up to dab a fingertip, smudge a wet

red smear between thumb and forefinger. A nervous glance left and right.

– We don't split up, he says. I've seen this movie, and we don't split up, right?

– Don't worry, kid, says Seven. The virgin always survives.

– Yeah, mutters Belle, it's usually the asshole who dies first.

– Or the slut, says Seven.

Eli ignores their bravado, gaze caught by a hobo sign scratched into tile over to his left. No Forgotten here now, but someone has been this way, chasing the same hope of hope as him, maybe? He wipes some of the muck off with his cuff.

– What does it say? asks Belle.

He's not sure. It's unusual, a hybrid of three signs. It might be nonsense, but maybe there's meaning in the combination, an attempt to say more than the crude language of survival is designed for. Maybe….

– It's not safe here, he lies.

– No shit, Sherlock, says Seven. Does it tell you where this Key might be? Or maybe the voices in your head know?

Eli answers by setting off down the left-hand path, the directionality of the sign one thing that's clear about it. He ignores their calls to wait, not even sure if he's leading the way or abandoning them. By the time they catch up with him he's already taken two turns marked with the same hybrid sign. He's already standing at the stairwell.

– Down, he says simply.

#

What Dreams May Come
They descend. A corridor, another stairwell, round a corner where—

Belle recoils. Things spew from nooks and niches, pale shapes of scar-flesh pink raining down to skitter into shadows, darting too fast to catch more than a glimpse, but that glimpse enough for her to see how they're malformed. Skin rats with bulging milky eyes in lumpen heads too big by far. Curled bodies, twitching stumps of tail. She doesn't let herself think what they look like, doesn't let the word *abortions* form as more than an unconscious sickening, a shudder down her spine. Still, this fucking place knows how to get under your skin, she thinks.

From somewhere ahead there comes a sound that might be a child giggling. Or not.

\#

They descend. Another level. A passage crammed with the junk of dead fairgrounds, jammed with—

Shit. The others tight in behind him, Seven picks his way through piles of broken automatons, carousel ponies and rusted hardware, kicking the door to each cell shut as he passes. No need to look inside, he figures, no need to see the things chained to the padded walls, jerking spastically from side to side, rocking back and forth with muted giggles, gagged moans, in their straitjackets and gimp masks. Shit. He isn't freaked by this House-of-Horrors bullshit—no way—it's just… he once saw knitting needles shoved up a snitch's nostrils… motherfucker took forever to die, crying like some retard, whining, no fucking idea what was happening or why. And glints of eyes peering out at them from the shadows now look just like that poor bastard's. Desperate. Mad. He can't shake the feeling that those eyes are staring right out of his worst memories.

Shit.

Seven kicks the cell door ahead of him shut and walks on.

#

They descend. A set of stairs, a corridor of doors, cell floors carpeted in—

Worms squirm on the stone, flaccid and flopping, squishing underfoot. Maggots drip from cracks in walls where leeches feed, tumescent, thick with a strange seeping ichor, white as milk and thick as pus. Pale centipedes snake over shapes in shadowed corners— creatures or corpses, you can't tell, the way they writhe. It's like they're walking into a wound, thinks Matthew, into something festering and infested. He follows close behind Belle and Seven, trying not to gag, trying not to think of childhood horrors, of waking screaming, retching, at the thought of a mouth choked with all the wriggling creatures of the earth, fat fingers of living filth filling his throat. He manages to hold the vomit down until they're out of it, until there's a solid wall for him to lean on as he spews his guts.

He feels a hand on his shoulder—Eli's.

– I used to have this nightmare, says Matthew, as a kid. It's like it knows.

– *What dreams may come*, says Eli. Maybe it does.

#

They descend, through chambers of walls so thick with ashen filth they look like earth, frayed wires trailing like roots, a sucking mire of gore and shit an inch deep underfoot. Blue bloated fingers curl round grills in doors long rusted shut, twitch as they pass. The noise is worse, though.

– Shit, says Seven. You hear that? This place is laughing at us.

– Sounds more like crying, says Belle.

Crying. Laughing. Eli can hear both in the sound, and more, a low chorus of sorrow rising to cacophonies of hysteria in broken rhythms, like some vast creature guttering endless last breaths in anguish. Stay here long enough, he thinks, and that mindless music could swallow you, drown you in a billion voices until one day you've forgotten what it's like to be sane.

– We're going to die down here, says Matthew. This place is going to eat us alive.

– We're already dead, kid, says Seven. Deal with it.

#

The Flesh Pit

– The sign pointed the other way, says Eli.

– This way leads *down*, says Seven. We're going *down*. So… *shit*.

Walls, floor, and ceiling of solid stone, the chamber Seven steps out into seems hollowed from the rock. With the scale of it, the balcony running round thirty feet or so up, floodlights and watchtowers in the corners—

– Place looks like a motherfucking prison yard, he says.

– After a riot, says Belle.

Bloodstains on the stone, dried and fresh. Fuck it, this has to be the way. Facing them, iron gates lie open across a dark maw of a doorway. They step out into the room—Seven first, Belle just behind him—all too aware of the sound in the distance—Matthew and Eli now—the echoes of howls becoming louder—all of them walking warily—a sort of keening, screeching—towards the centre of the chamber—rising, murderous, monstrous—turning to look around them—until the baying drowns out even Seven's shout of—

– RUN!

The storm of it bursts from the balconies first—broken forms of backward limbs swarming over the ceiling, tumbling, flooding down the walls—and then both exits—patched motley skin of iodine-yellow and shit-brown, scarred pink in stitching, scraped back to blood and bone—filling the room to a pit of flesh—misshapes of inhumanity. Seven is firing now, carving carnage into the coming waves that roll over each other, breaking in blood spray all around, but still coming, crashing down upon them all.

This is fucking crazy, he's thinking, fucking crazy, fucking crazy.

And *you* know that fucking crazy is *yours*, old friend.

\#

Hands paw and grasp, limbs lock around his own and Matthew feels fingers, lips, and tongues all over him as he flails, twisting to glimpse Seven swallowed in the mass, Belle hoisted overhead, passed back towards the dark gate. He sobs as he succumbs to the exultation of this sordid mass, something alien rising in his heart, a desire. A scream of joy.

It's not *your* fault, you tell yourself. It's not like *you* can help. Liar.

Then the boy is being dragged free by Eli, hauled out of the chaos of skin over muscle around bone, screaming and gasping as a surge of flesh carries Belle and Seven off through the other exit, into darkness, Matthew helpless, grasping.

– Move! roars the man in his face.

And they're moving, Eli dragging him along, out of the chamber, back to the other path of the T-junction, demons scrambling, scrabbling after. One turn. Matthew *realises* that they're running. Another turn. Realises what is behind them. Another. A doorway.

Eli shoves him through into a room. Then the door is shut, Eli toppling a filing cabinet across it as a barricade; but one of the things has made it into the room with them, and Matthew… Matthew is staring into its eyes.

It keeps crawling towards him even as he backs away, feels a rail at his back. It wants him to hold it, kiss it, fuck it.

He feels the pistol in hand, the kick of each bullet he puts into the thing's head, his finger still squeezing the trigger after that final *click*.

– We're safe, says Eli, for now.

But he'll never be safe again. He can't kill the part of him that... *knows*. That creature used to be a man and....

– We found it, says Eli.

– What? says Matthew.

Then Matthew turns, and the room finally registers on him.

#

A stone-dark sewer of a corridor, ceiling arched down into narrow walls: a stream of the grotesque, of bodies, hands, and faces, twisted and twisting, pours along it; and Seven is carried by the flow, arms wide, a cruciform crowd-surfer roaring with the river of gargoyle flesh. He knows that Belle is somewhere up ahead, downstream in the surge. He can hear her in the chorus. Gunshots and screaming. He doesn't fucking care, too busy spitting the slaver of his curses at them.

You want to help him. You really do.

His vision flickers like broken film: an opening into vaulted architecture; fivefold symmetries of fluted pillars; a small, dark space, some sort of chapel, lit as by fire through windows of bloodstained glass; a cross prepared for him. They raise him inverted, swarming up over silver sculptures to lash his feet, his hands. There are words in their babble—*lamb* and *shepherd* and *slaughter*, *blood* and *cleanse* and *sin*—but there's no more sense in them than there is in him as they drive the nail through his left hand with the butt of his own shotgun.

You think you could help him? You can't even help *yourself*.

Beneath him, they have Belle on the altar now, thrashing as they crowd in, tearing at her. One of them has his tongue out, drooling in her face, and she bucks, twists her head, savage as them, biting and spitting its own bloody flesh back at it.

Kiss this, you demon prick, you think.

– Kiss this, you demon prick, she snarls.

They don't need *your* help, you tell yourself.

Liar.

#

She doesn't know how it happens. Everything is blurred and broken, overlaid fast-forward and slo-mo images of wildcat fighting, gouged eyes and broken fingers, elbows in noses, knees in balls. She just keeps fucking fighting until she's on the floor under the altar and there's an Uzi in her hand. And then she just keeps on fucking firing until they're falling, and falling, and falling *back*. At the end of it, she finds herself as empty as the gun in her hand, standing staring at the barred door, at the charnel house around her, still empty as she clambers up, one foot on the cross, the other on the altarpiece of The Last Judgement, to free the hitman, lower the black messiah down from his crucifixion.

See, you think. They don't need your help.

Belle tears a strip from Seven's shirt to dress his wounded hand, looks up at his eyes as she wraps it round. Breaks the silence.

– So, do I even get a thank you? she says.

Seven flips the rosary hung round her neck.

– Whose Catholic shit you think this nightmare came from?

– Says a man who thinks he can take on all of Hell?

she says.

She squeezes his wounded hand.

– Shit, bitch. You ought to go into the dominatrix business.

– Screw that, she says. I think I found a new vocation.

She stands up, leaving the Uzi on the altar, scans the room to see if any more of their weaponry made it. Seven's shotgun lies beneath the cross, there's a pistol down beside the door, a ring on the floor in the centre of the room. She stops.

– What are you thinking? says Seven.

– I'm thinking catacombs, she says.

#

No More Down to Go

– It's got to be here, says Eli. It's got to be.

Matthew looks out over the iron railing, across the diameter and into the depths of a cavern of Babel, a hole of records; the room is a cylinder of vast dimensions, its inner wall one great gallery of filing cabinets that spirals round and down.

– You think the Key's down here?

He turns to see Eli working his way from cabinet to cabinet, fingers drifting over labels as he moves on, round and down.

– The Key? says Eli without stopping. The Key is a myth, a story.

Matthew starts following the man, slowly at first, then speeding up in time with Eli's search—fingers more frantic, his pace moving from walk to jog to run, cabinet after cabinet after cabinet, round and down.

– You told us the Key was the way out of here, says Matthew.

Eli keeps running, hands slapping drawers marked with dates and times, descending in seconds. Round and down.

– The way out to where? says Eli. Where is there to go? There's only one way out of here for sure.

Matthew is nearing his own death now, he realises, looking at one of the labels—the year, the month, the day, the hour, the minute, the second. Eli mutters to himself:

– They have to have found it. They have to be here.

If he's not looking for the Key, why is Eli even here?

– What the fuck are you looking for?

– Their paperwork, says Eli. Their death certificates.

#

Seven and Belle squeeze their way down the catacombs, a narrow spiral staircase walled with bone-framed alcoves, each crammed with corpse-matter. The empty stares of skulls. Skeletal hands twitch as they brush past. Every now and then they pass a low door leading into the darkness of a yet lower level. Their feet slip on the glistening steps underfoot, the stairway of ribs and digits fused into a grotto architecture of dissolved and accreted limestone, damp and dripping, slick and solid as if their way wound down through the inside of some vast stalactite. They try to picture the great chasm that stalactite might be hanging over, a hundred, a thousand other such stairway stalactites, maybe more. They can't.

You don't find it so difficult.

Every so often one or the other of them voices the doubt that they'll ever reach the bottom, that there even is a bottom. But what choice do they have? In Hell, all you can do is go down, until there's no more down to go.

So keep going, you want to tell them.

Another step, another step, and each one bringing them closer to that breaking of despair, that point where all there is to you, inside the automaton walking eternally down, is an endless scream of defiance. That's the madness that breaks most, you know, brings them to their knees, curls them up against the wall in a huddle, sinking into it, their scream dissolving into the echoes of a few billion others. Still, you have to reach that madness, you know.

The trick is just to keep walking through it.

\#

A city's worth of skyscraper floors, and forever more below, Matthew is stumbling after Eli, pleading with him to stop, just stop, when the hobo finally breaks. He staggers, grabs the rail for support, rattles it with white-knuckled rage, murder on his face as he roars the kid back from him. He whirls from the rail to attack a cabinet, wrench it from the wall and topple it, tear at it, sinking to his knees, a sobbing fury of fists and scattering files.

It's a purity of frustration you know all too well.

Matthew watches from a distance, helpless, crouches to pick up one of the cast-off files, a death certificate. One of the millions or billions who took the direct route out of Hell to God knows where.

Eli looks up at him, forlorn, a photo in his hand—a woman and child.

– I need to know where they are. I need to know if they....

And suddenly it all makes sense.

– What were their names? says Matthew gently.

Pull back now. See the boy down on his knees beside Eli as he coaxes the story out of him. See the tramp huddled in his arms, a tableau of grief and catharsis. And hush; let their voices fade to sobs and murmured solace. You don't have to hear this too-familiar tale of love and death. You don't have to hear Eli's tale of the deaths that shattered him to suicide, Matthew's confession of the desires he knows he's damned for.

All you need to know is this:

#

A million miles or a hundred hours from here—what does it matter in Hell?—down, down, and further down, a hitman and a hooker step out of one dark doorway to see, across from them, a hobo and a homo stepping out of another. Seven and Belle, Eli and Matthew, grimed in blood and eyes staring through each other, silent in their shared certainty—there are no outpourings of relief here, just a few grim nods and gruff words of greeting. As they come together quietly, turn to look down the corridor that leads out of the darkness, at the cast-iron arch at the end, at the furnace glow beyond, and the gantry disappearing into sulphurous smoke, billows of black, crimson, and gold, there's little need for in-depth discussion.

They walk out onto the gantry that stretches out across the lake of fire, glance back at two vast lead pipes on either side of the arch spewing waste that was once flesh, feeding the flames below with the rot of souls twice-dead, the dead of earth, the dead of eternity. They walk out into the acrid incense of Hell's furnace, a churning cloud so thick it's impossible to tell how far the lake stretches out to either side or ahead of them— maybe forever, they all think.

You know that's not true though, don't you?

You know just how close they are.

#

The Boardroom

A mere mile or two, a handful of hours—what does it matter in Hell?—a hitman, a hooker, a hobo, and a homo find themselves walking through another iron arch into a corridor of carved black basalt, cloisters cut into the rock itself, more corridors branching off. Clean lines and sharp corners, the place is calm and quiet as a monastery or a morgue, Art Deco uplighters on the walls, statues of angels at attention in alcoves. A voice echoes from up ahead.

– What? When?

Seven looks back at the others, a finger to his lips.

– Well, find them. Search every fucking sublevel.

He raises his hand, palm forward—*stay back*.

– I don't care. I want them stopped.

He follows the voice through the labyrinth, treading softly, the others following at a distance, slowing as the voice gets nearer—louder, clearer—until he's standing at a corner, peering round, down a short corridor that opens out into a room of black marble, a mahogany table in the centre of it, seats all round it, filled with… *things*, ancient rotted cadavers, someone's sick joke of a board of directors, thinks Seven. At the far end of the room, a glass cabinet is set into the wall, gleaming golden armour in it, a breastplate and a helmet, a shield and a sword, lit up like some museum exhibit. Under this, Seven clocks the shadow in the chair at the head of the table—a corpse just like the others, he thinks, at first, but chained and… *motherfucker*… *moving*, its head lolling forward, raising its gaze to look at him, this—

—drooling imbecile lobotomy golden warrior drenched in blood child torture victim screaming burning laughing beauty of burning cities and—

Shit! Motherfucker! Flat against the wall, Seven drags himself back to sanity, fights the nausea and panic, the sheer fucking *rapture* of terror; he doesn't know what that fucking thing is, and doesn't fucking *want* to know. It's all he can do to hush Matthew's *what is it?*

He swallows bile and turns back to the room.

#

– You couldn't get anything more out of them? OK, I'll be right up.

The owner of the voice comes into sight, a slick-suited shark in charcoal Armani striding round the table, cellphone in one hand, some strange ball of light balanced in the other.

– Yes, he says, kill them *all* if you must. So? Tell them the orders come straight from the very bottom. And don't fail me or I'll feed you to the Old Man himself.

He snaps the phone shut, stands behind the chair at the head of the table, leans over its occupant.

– Would you like a snack, old friend? You must be hungry by now, it's been so—

A church organ ringtone interrupts him; he flicks his phone back open.

– Hello? Yes, sir. I've already ordered the clean-up. No, it's all under control, sir. It's a shame to lose such an investment but—yes, sir. *Personally*, sir.

He hangs up, gives a humourless smile.

– I'll have to cut our chat short, old friend. Have to go. Orders from above. I'll leave this with you though, eh? I know how much it pains you to see it there, so near and yet so far.

He sets the glowing ball down on the table, spins it, stops it, then wheels and stalks off. As Seven listens to the fading steps, trying hard not to look at the chained thing, to keep his focus on the ball of light in front of it, one phrase echoes in his mind:

Orders from above.

#

Eli walks out into the room after Seven, Matthew and Belle behind him. That same phrase is echoing in all their minds, resonant with implications.

– What is this place? says the kid, but none of them

answer. In truth, it's all too obvious, this stillness at the heart of Hell with its committee of corpses and this... *being* none of them can look at without a sense of freefall into total madness. Visions of grace and horror, ecstasy and agony. Eli can feel them on the edge of his consciousness even as, on the edge of his vision, he sees the creature's head roll round towards the ball of light.

Help me.

He can't bear to look at it but, like the others, he can't help himself. He doesn't believe in it, never did, but what else could it be? What else would torture Hell's most important prisoner with its presence—so near and yet so far?

Little bit. Of Heaven.

Surely it has to be the Key.

A laugh. A scream. Two thousand years of bitter hysteria in a sob.

He can't help himself, his hand reaching for the light.

Please. Give it. To me.

Eli reaches past the claw of a hand, bound to the arm of the chair, palm-up and grasping. Feels his fingers curl round the ball. Both hears and doesn't hear the others, their noise without meaning—warnings or encouragement, he can't tell.

Please.

And then he's placing it in the grasp of the claw and letting it go, letting himself be dragged back from the shadow in the chair, the thing of madness, the being burning in its own broken mind, the flickering vision of millennia of insanity and torture.

The angel rising.

#

Steel shrieks and snaps around the creature's wrist, chains shattering from its arms and torso, as it stretches—

unfurls—into a stance. It sheds its bonds, shakes off captivity like some beast of the deep shambling to its feet in streamers of seaweed, ripping itself clear of centuries of detritus. It rises as a thing in flux, a flash-cut apparition in the strobing light of the globe it holds in one hand, a revelation of countless forms and faces, young and old, grotesque and gorgeous, images of flayed grace, mutilated glory, murdered beauty, crazed magnificence. Its mouth opens like a snake's, jaw dislocating to an impossible yawning openness to take the globe, swallow it like an egg.

One of them—it might be any of them—gives a panicked shout, something about a key. They don't understand what they're seeing, that the ball is only a bauble, a trinket, that it's what's inside that counts, the memories of a better place, a better time—before the Fall, you might say—those memories dissolving now, filling the creature's form with light. Restored, released, the angel rises, white wings unfurling behind it, form stabilising now as it throws off the shackles of horror with the last remnants of its chains, until….

Until it stands there, gazing at them with a glint of madness in its blue eyes but with sunlight in its hair and grace in its open hands reaching out towards them, the first of all archangels.

– Thank you, you say. I'm Lucifer, by the way.

#

Lucifer Unbound

– Sweet Jesus! says Belle.

You laugh in that way you know sounds… just a little crazy. Sweet Jesus? Yeah, too sweet for his own good. Nice line in socialist pacifism—sermon on the mount and all that—but too easily led, didn't figure it all out till the last moment. Father, father, why have you forsaken me? Poor schmuck.

– Sweet Jesus? you say. Not by a long shot.

– Hold on, motherfucker, says Seven. You're *the* Lucifer? The rebel—

You snort.

– I was his right hand, the captain of his host. Sir, yes, sir! I would have died for him. I loved him. Then one day I looked upon the face of God, looked him right in the eyes, all the way into his soul, and what I saw….

– Sent you mad, says Eli.

– So *someone* knows their apocrypha? Sweet. The truth *is* out there, you know.

But you must have been mad before, you know, to follow that bastard. Maybe you still are. Maybe—

Shut up. Just tell them what you saw.

\#

– You know what I saw? you say. Four thousand years of cities burning, inquisitions and crusades, jihads and pogroms. I saw Babylon fall, Sodom destroyed. Too many whores and faggots. You should see what he's got lined up for San Francisco, by the way. You saw New Orleans, right? Walk in the park. I mean, God forbid people have *a little fucking fun*, right?

You pace the room, look at what's left of your little corps of rebels, their corpses arranged in one of Gabriel's little jokes. At your old armour hung up as his trophy. At your reflection in the glass. You don't look too bad… considering.

You look fucking crazy.

Shut up.

– I looked into his eyes and I saw the truth, you say. And he… well, how do you like my personal gulag?

The kid bites his lower lip, summons the courage to ask:

– You didn't try to…?

– Overthrow him? you laugh. OK, so I thought

the world might be a better place without a murderous lunatic in charge. Yes, I tried to bring the fucker down. But if I belong here it's for service, not sedition.

– Nobody belongs here, says Matthew.

You smile.

– You can't imagine how glad I am to hear you say that.

#

You walk to the chair you've spent the last four thousand years in, get a grip on the back of it, lift it a little. It's pretty heavy, pretty solid.

– That wasn't the Key, by the way, you say. That was… my heart, you could say. I sort of lost it. Sort of had it ripped out.

– Then where *is* the Key? says Seven. 'Cause there better fucking be one, motherfucker, or—

– You humans, you say. So literal. You know how this place works. You've all figured it out… somewhere inside. It's fear and shame holds this place together, holds you in it. Despair and regret. Hell is the life you dream for yourself when you die, the one you think you deserve. You *think* you belong here, you *think* there's no way out, so that's how it is. Think about it, why don't you? The Key is *hope*.

And you take a running swing with the chair, slamming it through the glass of the display case, shattering it. You cast the chair aside, turn to smile at them one by one—Seven, Belle, Matthew, Eli. Hope is determination, you think. Hope is desperation. Hope is a yearning you can't deny. And hope is just plain old-fashioned insanity. You toss the helmet towards Seven, the shield towards Eli.

– Of course, hope is always better with a bit of backup.

You pick up the breastplate in one hand, the sword

in the other, hand one to Belle and the other to Matthew.
The boy looks at Seven.

– Maybe I'm not the best....

– Don't worry, Kitten, you say. That's the Mark I
Archangel Special. The original sword of fire. It's not
for close combat.

His nose wrinkles as he furrows his brow.

– Just point it and think *burny*, you say.

He holds it double-handed, stretched out at
arm's length, turns to face the empty cabinet, and—
searing, solid, the blast of fire that roars out makes a
flamethrower's jet look like a Zippo, smashing deep into
the wall, leaving a scorched crater.

– Neat.

– You'll find it's all in the wrist, you say. Loose and
limber.

You give the boy a wink, shake your hands with
fingers wiggling.

– Jazz hands, you say.

#

You lead them through the basalt maze. They're not happy
about going back the way they came, given that it means
facing the Twisted again. They'd be even less happy if
they knew about Gabriel's personal elevator, just a short
walk from the charred shell of the boardroom you left
behind you. Best not to mention that, you think.

– You really think you can get us out? says Belle.

– Have a little faith, you say. I have a Plan. It has a
diversion and everything.

You smile blithely at her over your shoulder as you
step onto the gantry. In the light from the lake of fire it's
probably not that reassuring.

– Look, trust me, you say. This whole place is a sort
of psychomimetic space, made to mirror the minds it
contains—and yours truly is the original test subject.

It was built around me, *for* me. I know it better than anyone.

– You've been stuck in that motherfucking chair, says Seven, in a room fuck knows how far below the surface, for the last four thousand years.

You look out into the smoke of dead souls, every swirl a shred of self whose end you've watched, suffered. Four thousand years of dreams of death, a pointed punishment.

– I have God's own cable, you say. In my head. Oh, yeah! Channel 24/7 piped direct to your nightmares. Reruns every second.

You giggle. It's really not funny, you know. Except it is, in a way. They're staring at you now.

– What? you say.

– Shit, says Seven. You even remember what it was like to be sane?

– Sometimes, you say. It was sort of like sunlight. Hurry up. We have a long way to go.

#

Taking Over the Asylum

Hell is for heroes, they say. OK. Picture an elevator door jammed by a gurney, its quiet *ping ping ping* suddenly joined by the rattle of gunfire getting closer, pounding feet and panicked screams; Matthew and Eli skidding round a corner, Belle and Eli close behind, guns blasting back the way they came.

– This is fucking crazy!

And you, bringing up the rear, grinning back at the horde of Twisted, slapping your thighs and yelling them on even as Eli pulls the gurney clear of the elevator door.

– *Come* on! Come and get the juicy souls! *Who's* a good demon?!

You turn and sprint, grab the sword from Matthew

as you pass, demons swarming round the corner behind you, Seven and Belle laying down a swathe of hot lead.

– Try not to kill too many, you say.

– The fuck?! yells Seven. Fuck you!

You slide to a stop where you have a clear shot at the stairwell, the door sealed in centuries of chains and padlocks, barricaded on both sides. One blast from the sword makes short work of it. Sure, it also bounces you off the walls and fills the corridor with smoke and rubble, but it does the job.

– Don't kill too many?! says Seven. You've got to be shitting me.

The hitman and the hooker are dragging you into the elevator now, still firing through the closing doors, at the Twisted swarming upon you now, over walls and ceiling and floor, pouring towards the fresh flesh of you all, reaching through the staccato spatter of bullets and blood, clawing for the gap that—

Closes with an utterly incongruous *ping*.

– See, you say. I told you I had a Plan.

#

Hell is other people, they say. OK, picture four humans staring at you as you stand in an elevator, humming *The Girl From Ipanema*, dancing your fingers in time, three steps forward, two steps back, up and down the buttons of the elevator. You hit the *hold* button at Sublevel 6 and they go crazy, babbling and blustering at you.

– What the fuck are you doing? says Belle.

Thing is, *they* can't see the Twisted pouring up the stairwell, spilling out onto each floor, rising, ever rising.

– Dead and pale and old and freaky, you sing.

The guards falling back in panic, stumbling up stairs, being dragged down into the chaos.

– The souls from Pandemonium go walking....

They can't see the faces, hear the shrieks, of utter terror.

– And as they're passing, each one they're passing goes—

– Aaaaaaaaaaaaah!

You dance your fingers up to the ground level button, twirl your forefinger above it, but halt and go for the emergency phone instead.

– Hello? you say cheerily. Maintenance? Is that maintenance?

You hold the phone out so they can all hear the sound of carnage coming down the line. Now they get the picture. Now they get the point.

You hit the button for the ground floor and the elevator rattles into motion again.

#

Hell is eternal torment, they say. A little part of you can't help but smile that Gabriel's thinking that right now, this very minute, as he stands over a blood-spattered guard, trying to ignore the window at his back, the sounds of commotion in the ER, people running past. Right now, he's thinking that maybe Lucifer's not the only angel God is punishing with this set-up.

– Are you sure you're telling me everything? he says.

His hands clamped to the man's temples, Gabriel gazes into rolled eyes, *deep* into them, *through* them. The guard is frothing at the mouth, no longer capable of much sense; it's something of an invasive procedure, after all. Not that Gabriel would get any pleasure out of that. He cuts his way through the man's mind.

– *Tell* me—?

A mangled corpse smashes through the window and Gabriel starts, turns, drops the juddering body of the broken guard. Outside, the ER is in uproar, guards and inmates scattering in his direction. What the…? He slams the door open, strides out into the mob of doctors, nurses, orderlies, patients all scrambling, clambering over each other, pushing past him, fleeing from….

The horde of Twisted sweeps into the ER, a wave of warped and fetid flesh.

– No, says Gabriel. No.

Stumbling, tumbling mortals thump and shudder him from all sides, trip him underfoot, stagger him back off-balance as he twists, struggles round to see the elevator doors slide open and four souls step out, four fucking faggot whore monkey-souls that should be fucking firefood already, their guns blazing hail upon the chaos. The fury is already roaring wordless in his mouth when the fifth steps out behind them, a form and face unmistakable… unimaginable.

It can't be.

You smile and wave at him as he's swept away in the rout of the ER.

#

– Move! you roar. This way!

You slam Eli through the swing doors into the ambulance bay, shove Belle and Seven after him, grab Matthew by the collar. He comes out of his rabbit-in-headlights daze, raising the sword of fire at the wave of Twisted streaming towards you, screaming a curse you never thought you'd hear from his lips, screaming it loud enough to drown out your *Not now!* The blast of angelfire sends the two of you backwards through the doors and rolling head over heels.

– Get in!

Seven hauls the boy to his feet and throws him at Eli, who's already hanging out the back of the ambulance. The hobo drags him inside as you roll to your feet, clock the situation. Belle leans out from the driver's seat of the ambulance, adding her voice to Seven's as she fires the engine into life. As Seven dives in the back after Matthew, you run for the passenger door, pull it open and—fold your wings in order to get inside.

– What the fuck? says Belle. You can *do* that?

– You've read your Bible, you say as she crunches the vehicle into gear.

The ambulance wheel-spins, tires screaming, then you're on the move.

– Angels have to pass for human all the time, you say. Not very easy with a fucking big set of wings on your back. Of course….

You lean out to look back, at the explosion behind you, the plume of smoke and fire, blood and flesh, the form leaping out of it now, landing in a crouch, coming after you at a sprint, great wings ripping out of its suit, unfurling and flapping, as Gabriel takes to the air, God's fire as a fury on your heels.

– It works both ways, you say.

#

ACT FOUR—SHOWDOWN

The Angel Gives Chase
— All units. Code 666 in progress at the Institute. Repeat, Code 666 in progress at the Institute. All units proceed immediately to—
— Fuck!

Gordon slams the brake and yanks the wheel hard as the ambulance tears across his path, the black-and-white spinning through a 360-degree skid. He ignores Kirkpatrick's curses from the seat beside him, still processing the image of *that bitch* behind the wheel when the great winged *thing* in the air rockets across the junction after the vehicle.

— What the fuck?! says Kirkpatrick.
— Gabriel, you say. Angel of fire. Angel of death. Who did you *think* would be in charge of Hell?

Seven leans forward between the seats.

— *You*, motherfucker, he says. Shit, man, you *are* the fucking—
— Source of all evil? you snort. Prince of lies? Sure. Fine. Whatever. Blame it all on the Lightbringer, as per usual. No, Lord, no. *We* didn't want to eat the apple. It was the *serpent* made us. He's bad, Lord, *mad*, Lord, tempted us with his subtle words of *rational thought*.
— Rational? says Seven quietly. Right.
— Knowledge of good and evil, you say. Damn it! Four thousand years and you *still* don't get it. I'm your metaphysical Deep Throat, man. The only crime I ever committed was to open your fucking eyes to the fucking—
#
— Carnage, shouts Knightly, carnage the like of which I've never seen. It's a riot, a rout, an eruption of wholesale

slaughter. And we're hot on its heels!

The Vox News reporter holds tight as the chopper banks hard round a corner. He leans in for a better view of the mayhem spreading out from the Institution, the crazed crowds, the trail of crashed cars.

– Men, women, and children, he shouts into the mic, fleeing for their lives, fleeing the terrible fury of the beast that lurks within us all, twisted with lust, the ravenous, ruthless, relentless force of base depravity! We're looking down on the true face of humanity here! We're looking down on—what the *fuck* is that?

– *That*, you say, pointing back at Gabriel. *That's* your prince of lies, right there. Three guesses who the king is, and I'll give you a clue for free: Ever hear of the Gnostic fucking demiurge? As for me, contrary to what you may have been told by—surprise, surprise—his loyal minions, I am *not* evil and I am *not* insane.

You clamber out of the seat and push past Seven, slap the sword of fire into Matthew's hand and a gun into Eli's. You kick the back doors of the ambulance open.

– Now, you say, are we going to toast the righteous and holy servant of Lord God Almighty, or what?

#

– Lucifer himself, says Knightly, the very prince of darkness in hot pursuit! Oh, the horror, the humanity. Surely these poor sinners will know no mercy, no hope, no escape from the archfiend bearing down upon them!

Over the angel's shoulders, between the pounding wings, Knightly sees the back doors of the ambulance swing open. He cranes forward eagerly at the sight of the hitman and the tramp on each side, the boy in the middle with... someone behind him holding his shoulders and... what looks like a sword in his hands. All three of them open fire.

– Oh, crap, says Knightly.

Bullets and angelfire rip the air, the angel weaving through it, left and right, swooping down, soaring up, up….

– Oh, *crap*, says Knightly.

You can't help but grin as the copter's undercarriage and Gabriel slam into each other with a *doom* you can hear from the street, the copter pitching and yawing wildly, spinning in the air even as the angel hurtles onwards and down like a ragdoll shot out of a cannon, ploughing into traffic and tarmac behind you with an impact that sends up a blast cloud of debris.

Seven, Eli and Matthew stare at you as you clap your hands in glee.

#

– Tell me we didn't just hit Lucifer, screams Knightly. Oh, fuck! We just hit Lucifer. Fuck! Jesus H. Christ and God Almighty! We just—*what? What?*

He turns to see the cameraman frantically miming *cut, cut*. Hears the producer screaming in his earpiece about the damn G-word. Crap.

– It's an idiom, he says, an idiom. I'm not invoking You-Know-Who. It's not—who gives a fuck? We just hit Lucifer!

He peers down at the intersection, at the pile-up of cars veering wildly to avoid the impact crater and the angel crawling out of it, the angel he just *knows* is Lucifer, clambering to his feet now, staring down the road, after the ambulance.

– Fuck, he's….

– …still alive, says Matthew. How can he still…?

– Angels are tough, you say. That would've just pissed him off.

Even as you speed away, you can hear the wordless growl of Gabriel's rage, feel the fury of his gaze as he flaps his wings wide, steps forward after you, entirely oblivious to the screeching brakes and blaring horn. You almost flinch as the yellow cab smashes into him. Almost, but not quite.

– As would that, you say.

#

Last Exit to Limbo

– Left here, you say. Left again. And left.

Treating the ambulance like a race car, Belle leans forward, one hand on the wheel, the other switching from gearstick to handbrake as she skids it round each corner, trying not to roll the thing but all too aware of the black-and-whites close behind, the copters above.

– What the fuck? says Seven. You're taking us round—

– Next left, you say.

– Motherfucker, we're going round in circles!

– And how! you say. OK, OK. Look, if we can make it to Limbo they won't come after us, won't cross the river into neutral territory—left again—and you'll *love* it there; it's peachy! Nice heathen crowd, all those unbaptised infants growing up without the Bible bullshit. Might be a little dull but—left here.

Belle yanks the wheel round, mutters under her breath.

– How can it *all* be left turns? says Matthew.

– Psychomimetic space, you say. Mirrors—

– the minds of blah blah blah, says Seven. Yeah, so?

– Haven't you kiddies learned anything since you got here? This is Hell, mister murder man. If it looks right, golly gee, it's *wrong*. Left here.

– There *is* no left here, says Belle.

– Oh ye of little faith, you say. And brake.

You lean over to slam Belle's knee down with one

hand, yank the steering wheel hard left with the other.

The world spins through a cacophony of horns and tortured rubber.

#

– Fuck!

Gordon hits the brakes, swerves the car to the right past the wildly spinning ambulance, crunching curb, thumping up onto sidewalk and skidding round to sideswipe a newspaper vending machine before finally— fucking thankfully—coming to a stop. Knuckles white on the steering wheel, heartbeat loud in his ears, he's looking back at… an empty road.

– What the fuck? says Kirkpatrick. Where the fuck did it go?

#

– You fucked-up fucking motherfucking maniac! says Seven.

The hitman struggles, murder in his eyes, gun in his hand, and Eli and Matthew on an arm each, trying to hold him back. Half off your seat, back to the door, you do your best to pacify him with your sweetest smile. It doesn't help.

– I'll fucking kill you!

– Look, says Belle.

She points straight ahead, through the windshield of the stationary ambulance. The others aren't paying her too much attention right now, though. Seven breaks an arm free, makes a grab for your throat.

– *LOOK!* she says.

And with one hand on your windpipe, Seven is just distracted enough to take a glance up… and then a double take. The ambulance sits in the scorched remnants of a park, black stone dereliction all round—Modernist towers, a Neoclassical mansion to the left—but it's the vast iron gate ahead and the spectacle beyond that holds his gaze: the great breach in the louring walls of skyscrapers; the dismal sky thick with smog; and the road leading out into it, rising towards the grey Gothic shadow of double arches and the ruptured spiderweb cabling of a suspension bridge.

– The bridge to Limbo, you say, and just a little set of gates to keep us from it. But I can deal with that.

You motion Belle out of the driver's seat, take her place and start revving the engine, handbrake on.

– You got another nifty left turn thing to get us past? asks Belle.

– Actually, you say, this is where the Key comes in.

You release the handbrake and the wheels scream bloody murder.

– Determination, you say, desperation, yearning, and insane faith. Oh, and….

You punch a fist through the windshield, clear a hole, and lean back to grin at Matthew.

– The sword might come in handy here, you say.

#

You crash through the gate in a blast of angelfire and ambulance, wreckage of torn steel scattering as shrapnel. You lean over the wheel, grinning like the fiend you are and singing a tune of triumph in death.

– Come on! you say. You all know this one!

Hell for leather, belting out the best of Steinman, you tear up the road, the bridge ahead a four-thousand-year dream of freedom finally realised. You weave through burnt-out cars, batting oilcans and garbage this side and that, take her up a gear as you hit the bridge proper, the road rising up to the great stone arches, disappearing into mist. The others don't join in the song, but what the fuck? If they don't care that the day is done and the morning's come and the sun's gone down and the moon outside is—

– Fool! says Seven. The bridge is—

Fuck fuck shit fuck brake fuck *brake* fuck *BRAKE!*

You slam on the brake, hold her straight as she yearns to turn, to flip; it's like you're trying to put your foot through the floor, dig your heel into tarmac, as the ambulance screams and shrieks and squeals and... stops.

Ten feet in front of you the bridge stops too.

#

A Void of Meaning

The ambulance at your back, framed by stone columns and cityscape, you stand at the bridge's end, a ragged jut of broken concrete and twisted steel extruding, warped and sheared, out into the grey. Matthew and Eli stand at your shoulders. Belle leans back against the ambulance, head lowered in despair. And Seven?

– Fuck! Fucking motherfucker!

Seven stalks back and forth, up to the edge and away, back again, fires a burst of gunfire out into the mist, drowning his curses. He pulls off the helmet, hurls it to one side.

– What if we find a boat? says Matthew. We could sail—

You shake your head.

– That's the Lethe out there, Kitten, you say. You'll dissolve like a toy ship in an acid bath—*sssssssss!*

– So fly us across, says Belle. You're Captain Superangel of the heavenly host. You could carry us, right?

– Two at a time, you say, express delivery, but....

– Then you take Eli and the boy first. Seven and I can handle—

– Fuck that, says Seven. Fuck that *go on without me* nigger shit. You flap those wings without me on your back, motherfucker, and I blow them off your fucking shoulders. Let the crackers stay behind. What?

– Very noble, asshole, says Belle. I save your sorry ass from getting nailed to a cross and you can't show a little team spirit? We'll draw straws.

You laugh. It gets their attention.

#

– You don't get it, you say. It's not just the water; it's the mist. The bridge wasn't there just to keep your feet dry. That was the only straight line ever made through that shit. Without it… round and round the angel goes….

– You're scared of getting lost in the fog? says Seven.

He curls a sneer at you, sniffs.

– That *fog* is oblivion, you say. That's a pea-souper of existential angst, a cloud of unknowing, a void of meaning. You can't feel it already, eating at your memories, making you feel a little… sketchy? If the wind was blowing the right way when you came in over the Styx maybe you caught a little scent of it before… not that you'd remember.

You crouch down to pull a battered license plate out of the dust, look up at Eli, Belle, Mathew.

– Pop quiz! you say. Any of you remember your last name?

You swing and spin, hurl the plate out like a discus, out into the grey, roll your shoulders as you turn to Seven.

– You even remember your *first* name? Wait for it.

They wait for a splash that doesn't come. One elephant. Two elephants. A spray of fragments and flakes blows back out of the mist, one larger scrap bouncing off Belle's breastplate with a *ting*. It lies at her foot, steaming.

– So we're fucked, basically? she says.

– Basically.

\#

Belle winds the ambulance through the remnants of the gate and parks it. In the rearview mirror, she can see Eli and Matthew following them down on foot, the angel behind them. Seven sits in the passenger seat, looking across at her, too damn quiet for her liking.

– What? she says.

She can see the judgement in his narrowed eyes, the sudden decision as he looks over his shoulder.

– Way I see it, he says, if hawkman there can't get us the fuck out of Dodge, well, we still have one big winged motherfucker of a bargaining chip. My guess is Gabriel wants him back pretty bad, but the rest of us... we're small fry.

So. He wants to cut a deal.

– You have a serious ethics deficiency, she says.

– Newsflash, he says. It's called self-preservation. You want to wait here for the motherfucking cavalry? How soon you think they'll come?

He's serious, she knows. As she watches the way he studies the others she can see the cold calculations in his eyes.

– And you're telling me this why? she says.

Because you owe me one, she thinks.

\#

– Because you're not a fuckin' nut-job, says Seven. Not yet, anyway.

He nods back at the fucking freak show behind them—the hobo wandering off to one side, talking to invisible friends again, the fucking crazy-ass angel throwing garbage off the side of the bridge—beer cans and rubble—dancing out of the way of the fragments that spray back. He's not going to end up like them, no fucking way.

So how come you can't remember your own fucking

name, Seven?

Shut the fuck up.

– And the kid? says Belle.

Matthew trudges towards them, hands shoved in his pockets. Shit, the kid might as well be kicking up autumn leaves 'cause his dog just died.

– Whitebread farmboy doesn't strike me as the betraying type, he says.

– And I do?

– You strike me as ready to make the hard choice. To survive.

She bites her bottom lip, plays with her rosary. He gives her the time, no pressure, no threat, no *breathe a word of this and you're history*.

– So what's your plan? she says eventually.

#

Under a Blue Sky

– So what's the plan? says Matthew.

Seven shakes his head. Belle just slams the door of the ambulance shut behind her. Matthew grabs her arm.

– There must be other bridges, he says. The subway map showed—

A hand on his shoulder stops him short—the angel.

– If Gabriel's closed the borders for good, he'll have closed them all.

Matthew shakes the hand off, rakes his fingers through his hair.

– Come on! There must be some way out. North? South? East? West?

– *West?* Kitten, that would be… ooh… monumentally audacious.

The pause catches his curiosity. And the phrase that doesn't quite mean *impossible*. It's something.

– Audacious? he says.

– Monumentally.

He gives a little lopsided grin. There's a little part of
him that's broken, he thinks, but he's not sure he doesn't
feel better for it.

– We just broke Heaven's Public Enemy Number
One from the depths of Hell. On a scale of one to ten,
what are we talking?

– That would be one and an itty bitty bit. This would
be off the scale.

#

– There *is* a tunnel, you say, to the west. You saw it
on the map, right? Well, it comes out *deep* in enemy
territory. Land of the pure, Kitten, home of the saved.
Oh, but it's *so* fucking beautiful. Golden fields, corn up
to your shoulders, wheat up to your knees, and a sky so
blue it puts your pretty little peepers to shame, Kitten.
Apple trees too, whole orchards of them.

They used to call it Elysium, you remember.

– Sounds like a nice place, says Matthew.

– It was creamy, you say.

Apart from the odd deicide now and then, you think.
Thou shalt have no other gods but me. Now hang 'em
high, boys! Swing 'em from the stars!

– What's the catch? says Seven.

– Even if we made it, you say, we're talking an
afterlife on the run, forever, in a place that hates you just
for who you are, *what* you are, a sinner.

– But we'd be *living*, says Matthew, under a blue
sky.

– Apple trees too, you say.

You leave it there, don't try to oversell it. You're not
really trying to manipulate them. Yeah, right.

Matthew shoves a hunk of gate with his toe.

– Anything's better than this, he says.

#

– We should ditch the ambulance, says Belle as she turns

the key, find something less conspicuous. The cops will
be—
– No, you say, we want to be conspicuous.

The engine growls into life. Seven climbs in the
back.

– How do you figure that?

– Mister Seven, you say, what do you do if someone
leans on you?

– I break his nose, says Seven, kick him in the balls
and, while he's lying on the ground, I put a bullet in his
kneecap.

Matthew jumps up behind Seven, leans out to call
Eli over from another of what Seven calls *his conference
calls with the crazy*. If only he knew what—hush, now.
Don't want them to hear, do you?

– Well, you say, that's how you deal with Hell. You
spit in its face, insult its mother, and tell it to bring it
on.

Belle sighs.

– You men with your pissing contests….

Eli finally clambers into the back of the ambulance.
He frowns at you.

– You want out, you say, you're going to have to
believe in yourselves, in each other. You're going to have
to *know* that nothing can stop you, fuck, that nothing can
even slow you down. You got to be doubtless, ruthless,
fearless. You want out, you gotta make *Hell* afraid of
you.

Belle puts her into first, takes off the handbrake.

– And how do we do that? she says.

– We break a few noses, you say.

#

Breaking Noses

Gordon kicks the black-and-white into reverse, thuds it
over the still-flailing corpse of the freaking monster in

a three-point turn and heads uptown. Kirkpatrick signs off on the call, hangs up the radio. Fuck, the streets are carnage every night but tonight it's the freaking Halloween Special, the bust-out beasts from the Institute tearing up the city as they spread through it. As if that's not bad enough, even the freaking street-scum are going crazy.

– Shit, did you see that? says Kirkpatrick. Upturned taxi. They took a fucking *taxi* out.

But Gordon's too busy gaping at the blast of angelfire roaring through the intersection ahead, and the ambulance that follows, siren blaring.

And what follows that.

#

Matthew whoops, taking out another parked car with a blast through the shattered windshield, swinging round to rip a shopfront apart with a bolt fired through the side window.

– This is awesome!

– This is fucked up, says Belle.

Another cop car pulls out behind them, siren wailing. Eli crouches at the open door, looking nervous.

– We seem to have got their attention, he shouts.

Beside him, Seven fires another burst at the trail of black-and-whites.

– You don't say, he mutters.

Above and behind them, you beat your pinions, roaring louder than a thousand rivers:

– GABRIEL!

#

But elsewhere, on the roof of the Institute, the Lord Fucker of Hell is busy. He stalks through the smoke belching up through the blazing building, juggling calls on his cellphone, switching from murderous rage to crawling obsequity as he taps the button to switch from this call to that:

    – Which way are they headed? [tap] Yes, sir. Absolutely. [tap] You're sure of this? [tap] No, sir. That won't be necessary. [tap] Then send more cars! *All* of them! [tap] I don't know, sir. They're heading west but—no, sir, that would—I'll make sure of it, sir. [tap] What? Who gives a fuck about the *taxis?* [tap] No, sir, we don't need reinforcements. [tap] Well, *let* them riot. We'll deal with that *after.* [tap] Yes, right now, sir. Bye, sir. [tap] Just gather everything we've got at the Tunnel. I want every man still standing waiting for them at the Tunnel. Let the whole fucking city burn. Let it burn.

\#

Hell in a handbasket of glimpses: streets filled with flaming wrecks and fleeing citizens; filth geysering from broken hydrants; a barricade of burning taxis; rioters throwing bricks and bottles at armed police; a fire engine on its side; citizens atop it holding off a mob of Twisted with flamethrowers; cops hung from traffic signals; gangs sweeping into the business district; looting and lunacy; blooms of flame and glass from office windows.

    You soar up in a spiral out of the concrete canyon, rising above it all to circle a spire that spikes the sky, survey the cityscape of pandemonium. Uptown, rockets streak into the sky, one taking out a police copter—pretty fireworks, and just for you.

    You let the updraft hold you up for a second, for a beat of wings, a grin, then dive back down into the city of destruction.

\#

Breaking News

– We're closing in on it now, says Knightly. What've you got for me?

    The Vox News copter sweeps left as he listens to

the producer's update. A hitman, a hooker, a hobo, and a homo—that all checks out. Word on the street is they made it down to the lowest depths of the Institute. And brought something back with them. No fucking way.

– The Key? says Knightly. But if it *is?* What do you mean, *we can't?* This is the fucking story of the century! Don't be a fucking pussy. That's not going to happen. When these idiots fail, it'll be *triumphant!*

He's still trying to sell the story as the greatest put-down in Hell's history when a thud shudders the copter and he fumbles the phone. There's a creak, a crunch, then the door of the cabin is ripped open and—shit—wind from the blades roaring round him, an angel reaches in to grab a camera from a shocked cameraman's hands.

You flick him a salute as you kick off into a backflip.

#

– Incoming! yells Seven. Move!

He shoves Eli back and slams himself out of the way as the angel comes in like a meteor, aimed straight at them, wings folding, tucking and rolling—fuck! Lucifer crashes in through the open doors, impact jolting the ambulance, tubes and meds tumbling around him. He comes up dishevelled, a camera in his hand.

– What the fuck are you doing now? says Seven.

The angel hushes him, fiddles with the camera for a second, then holds it up at arms reach, grinning into it.

– And we're back, he says. This is Lucifer Morningstar, coming to you from a speeding ambulance. Around me a ragtag crew of brave souls united by their scorn for Hell's dominion. A murderer, a fornicator, a sodomite, and a suicide. Damned! Doomed! Deviant! *Defiant!* Do you have a message for our viewers, Mister Seven?

Seven flips the finger at the camera or the angel—

he's not sure which.

#

Knightly scrambles over the seat back, grabs headphones from the sound guy and swings the monitor round for a better view of the feed. This is fucking gold dust!

– Patch it through, he shouts. Patch it through.

The producer's still on the phone, babbling incoherently about the Powers-That-Be and how it can't be Lucifer and none of this makes sense.

– Fuck it! snaps Knightly. Who *cares* what's going on. This is chaos, baby! This is what Hell's all about, and we've got a live feed right in the centre of the action. Television history? Baby, this is television *eternity!*

#

Eli fires another rattle of gunfire randomly, aiming at street signs, kiosks, the air, *anything* as long as it's not human. He's not a killer, *won't* be, not even here. Across from him, Seven shows no such compunction, aiming for tires and windshields, drivers, whatever's still moving on the sidewalks.

– And this man, the angel is saying, this man here, whose only crime was to love too much, who harmed no-one but himself in a tragic suicide—

– Eli! Matthew yells back from the front. Seven! Get up here!

Eli doesn't need an excuse. He stumbles up front to peer past the boy, see what's spooking him. Ahead, the crosstown street is a narrow crack bridged by high walkways and terminating in the louring bulk of a tower-block, a dark maw at its base. Around the entrance to the tunnel it looks like half of Hell's police force is gathered for the roadblock.

#

The Tunnel

– There's too many! yells Matthew

Another bolt of angelfire hits the frontline of police, takes out two cars and a wall of sandbags. Squeezed in between them, Seven's Uzi spits slaughter into the cops, but it's not enough. Beside him, Belle is turning the word *cunt* into a mantra. Behind him, Eli—is being shoved aside by Lucifer.

– More power! shouts the angel.

– Yes, says Matthew, we need more power. And just how—

– Kitten, you're still thinking *burny*, says the angel. You need to turn it all the way up to *boom*.

The flicker of firelight in his eyes doesn't fill Matthew with confidence but as they bear down on the wall of authority there's no time to doubt. Matthew points the sword forward, holds it tight, and *thinks boom. Big* boom.

The fireball rips a path twenty feet wide through the roadblock.

#

The ambulance blasts through ash and splinters of torched cops and barricades, launches itself into the air and comes down with a crunch onto a road of broken glass, burning oilcans, hulks of dead army trucks. It skids this way then that, sideswipes a tollbooth as Belle struggles to weave a safe path at this speed. In the rearview mirror she sees the angel swoop to follow them into the slalom of car wrecks, camera in one hand tracking them as he banks left and down, sweeps up to the right, like a fucking jet fighter dodging flak. Shattered tarmac and scorched walls, ruins of Humvees and jeeps, the tunnel looks like a war zone, like some fucking convoy ambushed by insurgents or blown to fuck by friendly fire, but there's no time to think what it all means. Ahead of them the way is blocked by a pair of trucks, one on its side, and beside her the kid is raising the sword of fire to clear the way.

She barely has time to shout, No!

#

– Nice aim, says Seven. You trying to bring the fucking roof down on us?

He scrambles up the slope of rubble and half-buried vehicles after Matthew and Belle.

– We can still get through, says Belle. Give him a break.

Seven growls as he reaches the top. So the blast didn't block the tunnel completely. It's cold comfort.

– If we can make it, so can the cops, he says. And without the ambulance we're fucking sitting ducks. Or lame ducks.

Below them, Lucifer reaches a hand back to Eli. The two men exchange some quiet words. Eli nods back towards the mouth of the tunnel, says something else. Two bullets right now might not be such a bad idea, thinks Seven. It's only the potential leverage of the angel holding him back, he tells himself. That's what he tells himself.

#

– We're close now, says Lucifer.

Half an hour or half a day, it's hard to tell how long they've been winding their slow way onwards, sword of fire held up as a torch in Matthew's hands, lighting debris in the darkness. Eli glances at the shadows and the things that lurk there unilluminated, but he can only really see them in the corners of his eyes. If the angel's sight is clearer he doesn't show it, focusing the camera on the barricade of cars and sandbags, six feet high across their path. It's hard to tell how long they've been in the tunnel, but it seems like they've been going up now almost as long as they were going down. Almost.

– You smell that fresh air? says Lucifer. That's

freedom. Babies, I can almost taste it. Don't you just want to grab it and take a big juicy bite?

The reply that comes from up ahead is smooth and smug.

– More temptations, Lucifer? Four thousand years and you still haven't learned your lesson.

#

The Gates to the Garden

A hundred yards of black no man's land leads up to another barricade backgrounded by grill-hatched light and shifting silhouettes—the gated exit from the Tunnel and the forces guarding it. Freedom blocked by iron and blood. You don't need a clear view to know how many Gabriel has called in to stop you. You can feel their animal fear and human hatred, every twitching finger on every trigger of every gun trained on you as you stand on your wall, facing Gabriel on his. Four millennia and little's changed, you think, except the armies at your backs. It's hard not to remember that this is where you made your last stand, but you try your best.

– You can't possibly think you're getting out of here, he says.

– You can't possibly think you can keep us here, you say.

#

Gabriel laughs. God's bootboy is armoured up now, you can see, breastplate, shield, and helmet gleaming with reflected glory. His sword of fire flicks through the air, taunting.

– You keep yourselves here, he says. You should know that most of all, Lucifer. You stay because you belong, because it's all you have left. You made your choices. You made this place.

Dust of concrete and ash, battle lines of rusted steel and sandbags, men with guns instead of wings and armour—still, beneath it all, you can sense the shadows of the ancient dead burned into black rock walls of a tunnel carved by angelfire. A retreat leading to defeat.

– You dug your own grave, says Gabriel. We just filled it in.

#

His voice echoes over the murmur of the guards behind him, Seven and Belle whispering below. You can feel the hitman's gaze on the back of your neck, hear the clicking logic of his thoughts. A bullet in the shoulder to bring you down while you're not looking, a gun at the back of the head, Belle holding back Matthew and Eli while he strikes the deal.

Not yet, you think.

Not yet, thinks Seven.

– *And they saw that they were naked*, calls Gabriel, *and were ashamed*. And they still are, Lucifer. Look at the eternities of shit they make for themselves, the shame, the self-loathing. You really didn't think they'd use the knowledge of good and evil to judge themselves?

– I gave them the truth, you say.

– You gave them the fire of their own damnation.

#

– They were warned, he says. *Eat of the fruit and you shall surely die*. And what great secret did they get for it? That good and evil don't fucking *exist*. We make them up as we go along.

Even with the camera zoom on max, from a hundred yards away you can't quite see his sneer. It doesn't matter though. Nothing does.

– And did they surely die?

You turn the camera on Seven just as Eli's hand clamps on the hitman's gun arm.

– On the day you first knew what it meant to murder, did you die?

You swing it round to Belle.

– On the day you first had felt *whore* cut into your heart, did you die?

And then you swing it round to face the lens, to speak to anyone in Hell who's watching… which should be pretty much everyone.

– Any of you, all of you….

#

A Hope in Hell

This is Hell: a city of people watching televisions in squalid homes, hotel and hospital rooms, swarming the streets in front of shop windows, gathering under vast screens in the square at the heart of the entertainment district; fighting and fucking and feeding on the 24/7 spectacles of Vox News; the daily revels and rituals of riot and rape, and now new horrors unravelling; a three-day story of Hell *truly* unleashed; breakouts and break-ins and fugitives on the run but bound, baby, *bound* for the best fucking doom you ever saw; that doom never coming though, just a fucking circus show of angels and fireworks; four survivors fighting their fucking way to the very fucking gates; an angel's face in a grainy straight-to-camera shot; the most wicked grin anyone has ever seen.

#

– On that day, you say, when you first looked at yourself in the mirror and saw the truth you couldn't handle, did you die? Or just crawl away and hide, bury that truth, cover it up? Fig leaves and fucking self-delusions. You think you deserve this? OK. You do… for fucking wasting what I gave you.

You let loose four thousand years of bitter fury at their betrayal, your own folly. If they want to burn in Hell, let them burn completely.

– You want a crime to torture yourself for, try

cowardice. The only sin that ever mattered a shit is the shame that put us all here. Fuck, I didn't give you that power just so you could judge *yourselves*. I gave you the power so you could judge *God*.

– No one judges God, shouts Gabriel. You don't have the right.

– I say we do.

#

This is Hell: a surge of crowds moving through the streets, converging at junctions, sweeping in from the north and south, heading west towards the tunnel, a mob wild with murder but focused on a single target, not themselves, not each other, but the place itself, this prison pit with its source inside their poisoned hearts, oh, but its surfaces outside, every wall a mirror to smash, every street an artery to slash. There are plenty out there who still don't get it, you know, who never will, but those who do drag the others in their wake. Fuck the slow suicide of the soul; this is a million madmen so wretched they're ready to take a hammer to the last pretence of reason.

Hell can break any man, you know, or any angel. Or any God.

#

Gabriel turns to speak with someone behind him. You almost feel sorry for him. He'll be getting the report right now, and he still thinks he can stop you.

– It won't work, he shouts. You don't have—

– *a hope in Hell?* you cut in. Baby, I *am* the hope in Hell. I'm the bringer of light, Gabriel. And the odds are on my side.

– A murderer, a whore, a faggot, and a lunatic, he says. I'll have ripped your wings off and eaten your fucking heart long before your little army of monkeys gets here. I would have done it centuries ago, but He wanted you to suffer.

– Baby, you say, my army's already here.

And you pan the camera around the tunnel, behind you and ahead of you, at the darkness which only the viewscreen shows as filled with ragged shades. Gabriel looks at you for a second, then down at the ground below him, then back at you.

Then the Forgotten are upon him.

#

Now or Never

The angel whirls like some mechanism in a storm of torn time, broken space, shield slamming blurs of shades away, sword slashing through the churned air. Bodies and scraps of bodies fly out of the maelstrom, membered and dismembered as he twists and turns, slices his focus through them. There's no doubt Gabriel can hold his own against a few Forgotten, but if the gunfire's anything to go by, well, his minions aren't doing quite so well. Crouched on the barricade beside Lucifer, seeing slaughter manifest before them, shades made flesh, forms coming clear, Eli grips the shield. It's now or never.

Behind him, Belle is shouting, Seven is cursing, and the boy is scrambling to drag him back to cover. A stray streak of angelfire scythes wildly overhead, but Eli pays it little mind.

– And so, he says, lest they eat also of the tree of life and become as Him, therefore the Lord sent them forth out of Eden.

He stands up, gun hand rising to take aim.

– And he placed before the gate an angel with a sword of fire.

As the angel turns to stare straight at him, he gets the one clean head shot that he needs.

And then the sword swings and his world is fire.

#

Matthew doesn't see how badly Eli's hurt, just the ragdoll body flying back over his head. Then he's up and over the barricade, landing and sprinting through a scattering mob of things he can't quite see, flashes of arms and shoulders, glimpses of faces, echoes of voices nearly drowned out by his own roar. The sword in his hand is blasting—bolt after bolt of angelfire like bullets, tiny and precise—but the angel ducks, deflects; he just can't hit the bloody—

He's still blasting when the angel hits him, not with fire but with his shield, a dive and body-slam that sends him sprawling, stunned. He tries to drag himself upright, but he's still on his knees when the arm locks round his throat, hauls him up, dangling and flailing... choking.

– Hush, Gabriel hisses in his ear. I know it hurts. I know it's hard.

The angel fights on with Matthew clawing at his arm. He spins the boy as a human shield, the sword of fire flicking through a haze of motions, blurs of forms. It doesn't make sense. It can't end like this.

– I know you're wondering, says Gabriel, how can you die if you're already dead, how can I kill you if you're already in Hell?

Matthew's chest heaves with the panic of choking, the terrified lurch of denied gasps, sobs refused.

– Ask yourself how can you live in a place like this? How can you live as what you are? How can you live at all?

There are other sounds, glimpses of sights in his blurring vision, but none of it makes sense.

– The answer is you can't.

After a while the flailing stops.

#

As Gabriel lets Matthew's body drop, Belle and Seven open up a hail of gunfire on the bastard from the barricade, but he darts this way and that, bullets bouncing off his armour. Beside them, Lucifer keeps on filming.

– Fuck this, says Belle.

She drops to the tunnel floor and runs for the angel, firing high, low, left, right, anything to get past his shield. She swings sideways to dodge a bolt of angelfire, ducks another with a roll, and—fuck, yeah—gets a bullet in his shoulder. Then she's inside his guard, straining to get her gun into the fucker's face. But he's too fast; she feels a wrenching pain in her wrist, arm, shoulder, air under her feet. Then she's flat on the ground, staring in his ice eyes as he brings the sword to bear on her. *Fuck, she's—* Seven slams into the angel, one hand clamping on his wrist and twisting hard. The sword goes flying, but the angel sweeps his arms to break the hold, lock Seven in his own. A head-butt hard enough to make both helmets ring sends the hitman staggering back. Belle dives for the fallen sword, but again the angel's too fast. Even with the breastplate, ribs crack audibly as his boot sends her flying, rolling. We're all going to die, she's thinking as the bastard crouches to retrieve his sword. He's going to kill us all.

The fucker's even smiling at her when a blur of flesh and feather by the name of Lucifer smashes him full-force through the barricade and into the clash of Hell's anointed demons and forgotten souls.

#

You fight as fury and fate, a wildcat frenzy of fists and feet, an elbow in the ribs, knee in the groin, wings beating. Locked or loose, you spin, attack to defence, defence to attack. His helmet's in your hand, ripped off. His teeth snap at your ear. You slam a forearm in his face. Together you spin and weave through blows blocked and landed. It's not capoeira or karate, just kill-crazy brawling aimed at bloody murder.

All you want is to spit your last breath in his severed head's slack jaw.

Because he's everything you used to be.

And then you have him with a fist that pounds into his solar plexus, punching the air out of his lungs and bringing him to his knees: Your hands clamp round the fucker's face; thumbs press into his eyes, squeeze hard; nails gouge; thick rubbery tissue holds, and yields, and splits, vitreous humour bursting out onto your hands. You keep pushing till you reach the blood.

Gabriel screams, arms whirling, scrambling upright as you step back, flick the gore from your cramped thumbs. He's half-swamped in the Forgotten before you even turn away.

#

Score One for Sodom

Was it ever possible they'd all make it out? *Really* possible? Seven clambers to his feet, stumbles over to where Belle is on her knees, leaning over Matthew's lifeless body. It's a dark and bitter pietà, the scene, with bloody-handed Lucifer walking back towards them through the broken barricade, behind him the archangel swallowed by an angry mob of Hell's Forgotten, every man and woman of them visible now. Membered. Eli gazes at the gates beyond, the light hatchworked by iron. At the boy.

Scorched shield still in his hand, Eli scrambles down sandbags to the tunnel floor. There's no tears in Belle's eyes as she looks up at him. Whatever emotion he can't read in her face is too complex for that.

– The kid had heart, she says hollowly. That's what they say, isn't it?

#

Seven's hand goes to her shoulder, squeezes. It's not that he gives a fuck about her, or the kid, no, it's just… it's just too damn motherfucking *bullshit*. Hell in death and death in Hell. The boy had fucking heart alright, a heart to be stopped, breath to be smothered, life to be—wait.

Heart, you think. *Breath*, you think.

Seven turns on Lucifer, brows furrowed in anger and demand.

– How can you die in Hell? he says. How can you die when you're already dead?

– If you've got a mouth to talk, says Lucifer, if you breathe….

– Then… fuck!

Seven pulls Belle clear, drops to his knees over the kid, to clasp his hands on top of Matthew's chest and pump, without craft or calculation, with only the rhythmic count of his motherfucking bloody-minded determination.

– Someone help me, he says, for the love of fucking—

– Humanity, says the angel at his side.

And as Seven counts the beats, drives them into the boy's heart, Lucifer leans in over the kid, his mouth to Matthew's, to blow breath into his lungs.

#

A ragged gasp, the tearing rasp of air, of life ripped from a world of death. The boy coughs, gasps again, and then he's breathing, chest rising and falling. Human hand or angelic breath, it's a fucking miracle, and Belle laughs at the wonder of it. The pain that spears her side might cut her joy short with a curse, a dizzy stagger, but it's fucking worth it. It's all fucking worth it. For the first time Lucifer's smile doesn't seem completely crazed. A little sly, like he knows something they don't, but not like what he knows is how to guard your thoughts from God with a tinfoil hat. It might be the first time she's seen Seven and Eli smile at all. She looks at Matthew's face, eyes closed but breathing, colour slowly coming back. At the blood and the bodies and the limbs around them. At the two angelic swords lying in the gore.

– So are we getting the fuck out of here or what? she says.

#

It doesn't make much sense to him at first, but as things coalesce into awareness, Matthew blinks, raises a heavy head, and slowly finds his focus. Eli and Seven have an arm each, hauling him between them. Belle leads the way ahead, a sword in each hand, through a crowd of tattered men and women, hundreds of them, parting to make way. He drags his feet into a stumbling walk, looks back over his shoulder to see Lucifer behind them. And more souls in ragged layers, many stained with blood, stretching back into the darkness. He doesn't look down at the things he's tripping over, slipping on.

They stop. He croaks a sort of question and Belle turns, steps to one side. Back to the gate, his shredded wings stretched wide, his naked flesh smeared red with blood, Gabriel spits and hisses, thrashes at enemies beyond his reach. Matthew stares into the horror of this mad thing's hollow sockets. He struggles loose from Eli and Seven, lurches up to Belle. She hands him the swords before he even asks.

Weak on his feet but stronger than he's ever been, he raises both swords, rips three agonising words out of his throat.

– Kiss. My. Ass.

And hits Gabriel with the full force of doubled angelfire. Set to *raze*.

#

Going Home

You walk out into a strange world, not at all what you remember. What was once riverbank is now a vast concrete buttress rising at your back, squat turrets all along it. What was once the wildwood edges of Elysium is now a line of white sand dunes, rising to the same height as the buttress and running parallel to it, north and south as far as you can see. The road out of the tunnel disappears into those dunes, buried in four thousand years of oblivion. How far they carry on, you don't know; this isn't your domain, not now, anyway. He might have levelled the whole afterlife and sown the ground with salt, all but His own little kingdom.

You're waiting for the questions. Where are the green fields? The apple trees? But none of them speaks. They just stare past you… not at the dunes but at the sky above them. The clear blue sky.

Maybe it's not all lost, you think.

#

– Indomitable, rants Knightly, inexorable, incredible, our conquerors of Hell have won their freedom! Hell has truly broken loose! Yes, people, it's a victory for hope, for justice, everything that's pure and good and right. And we at Vox News are here to bring you the story of that victory.

As the chopper flies out over the skyscrapers on the western edge of Hell, the buildings of the city locked tight into a single solid wall falling sheer into the Styx, Knightly hears the producer in his earpiece.

– Knightly, you're entering the No-Fly Zone.

He ignores it. No one's going to stop them now. He waves the pilot on, rolls a hand for the cameraman to keep filming. Across the misty water, the far shore is a line of grey concrete and white sand, black specks just about visible on the dunes, spreading out from the tunnel's exit.

– Knightly, the guns aren't manned. They have an automatic targeting system, radar….

But Knightly is too busy trying to spin a new role for himself.

– This is the story of a plucky band of individuals, he says, of heroes fighting against all the odds, against their fates, against... oh, shit.

#

From the ridge of the dune, you look back at the island city of Hell, the rag-toothed island of ashen ruin, shrouded in mist, almost lost in the louring sky. At missiles streaking up from the turrets of the buttress. At the Vox News copter exploding in the sky. Below you, Seven gives a low whistle.

– We made it, he says.

– That we did, says Eli.

– Monumentally audacious, says Matthew. I reckon that's the phrase.

You don't tell him the monumental part is still to come.

– So where do we go from here, birdman? says Belle.

You smile, point a thumb over your shoulder, relish the looks on their faces as each steps up high enough to see what's over the rise. You turn.

#

The dunes stretch for miles, maybe hundreds of miles, but beyond them there's the green of fields and trees and, beyond that, far off in the distance, across the great empty plains of the afterlife, great towers rise on the horizon, a city of shining silver, glittering gold.

– Don't know about y'all, you say, but I'm going home.

And you look back at them, and at the ragged hundreds who were once Forgotten clambering up the dunes after you, at the thousands more now pouring out of the Tunnel, spreading out, at every sorry citizen of the infernal city unleashed, and many, you're sure, with only one thought on their minds after escape from Hell: assault on Heaven.

– Who's coming with me? you say.

One by one, Seven and Belle, Matthew and Eli— even Eli—they nod.

ABOUT THE AUTHOR

Hal Duncan was born in 1971, brought up in a small town in Ayrshire, and now lives in the West End of Glasgow. A member of the Glasgow SF Writers Circle, his first novel, *Vellum*, won the Spectrum Award and was nominated for the Crawford, the BFS Award and the World Fantasy Award. The sequel, *Ink*, came out last year. As well as publishing a poetry collection, Sonnets For Orpheus, he collaborated with Scottish band Aereogramme on a song for the Ballads of the Book album from Chemikal Underground, and has had short fiction published in magazines such as *Fantasy*, *Strange Horizons* and *Interzone*, and anthologies such as *Nova Scotia*, *Paper Cities* and *Logorrhea*.